Broken Idol

The Billionaires' Club Series: Book 6

AE Moran

The Invisible Publishing Company

The Billionaires' Club Series

Contents

Chapter 1: Giovanni

My eye scans the room when I stroll into the nightclub. Scantily clad girls pack the dancefloor all undulating their bodies to the deep bass of the dance music.

A bunch of losers in jeans and T-shirts slouch around the bar. They're all guys and they're all alone—of course. None of the girls go near them.

I straighten my shirt cuffs and pull them down to the right distance past my jacket sleeves. I look damn good in a perfectly tailored Tom Ford suit.

If anyone is going to go home with any of those girls, it will be me—not some construction worker who doesn't know how to dress.

I saunter into the room taking in the atmosphere. Couples line the railing above the dancefloor. Half the girls here are single. The other half stay near their boyfriends or whoever they've paired off with.

I try to pick out which girls I like the best, but I have to pay attention when I walk across the room to join a different group of guys standing together. They all wear suits, too—and they look great.

None of these guys is a member of The Billionaires' Club, but they're all in the multi-million range and climbing. They'll get there sooner than later. Then they'll become members.

These guys are also my age. They're the only men my age that I can talk to about business and money. The only other club members my age are Rory Kahn and Niko Holloway.

They'll talk to me about business and money, but things changed between us after Niko got married. He was never much of a ladies' man before that. Now he's married and doesn't have time to enjoy the opposite sex the way I do.

I only make it halfway to my friends before four girls notice me and come over. They flank me on both sides and run their hands all over my jacket.

"Hi, Giovanni," a strawberry-blonde purrs in my ear.

"Hello there, Helena." I smile down at her. "Where have you been hiding out?"

"I've been looking for you." Her eyes widen. "Are you seeing anyone special tonight?"

"Yes, I am. I'm seeing you." I slip my arm around her and kiss her on the neck. She feels silky soft and smells of perfume....and something else.

She laughs. Another girl slips her hand under my jacket and strokes my sides through my shirt. "What are you in the mood for tonight, Giovanni?" she asks. "My friend and I are looking for someone who wants to have a threesome."

I have to tear my attention away from Helena. This second girl is darker with sultry black eyes and sweeping, wavy black hair spilling over her bare shoulders.

I've seen her around before. Her name is Rhianna. Her shimmering silver dress somehow makes her eyes and bright red lips look even brighter.

"Is that so?" I ask. "Where's your friend?"

"I'm her friend." The third girl comes right up to me from the front, glides her arms around me, and then runs her hand up my thigh to touch me through my pants.

She has dark brown chestnut hair and green eyes streaked with bright radiating lines. Niko is the only other person I know who looks like that, but this girl's eyes don't look predatory or dangerous. She looks intoxicating.

Her touch makes me hard right away. I can't stop staring at her. I want to grab her right now and force her down on her knees, but I can't do that with my arms around two other girls.

She runs her hand up and down my length while she murmurs in my face. "You like that, don't you?" she breathes.

"Yeah, baby," I growl back. "You know you want it deep and hard, don't you? Is that what you want? Do you want me to give you that?"

She pretends to cringe while she teases me to the breaking point. "I need it so bad! I need you to give it to me."

"Wait your turn, Lydia," Helena snaps and yanks Lydia's hand away. "I had him first."

"He said he wants to have a threesome," Rhianna points out. "He can't get that with you."

"Now, now, girls," I tell them. "There's no need to fight over it. Why don't all four of us go home together? I'm sure I have enough in my tank for all of you."

Helena frowns. "Are you sure about that?"

"Do you have a problem with that?" I kiss her again. "I'm sure I can take care of these girls and you at the same time. I've done it before."

She blushes and smirks at me. "Okay. That sounds fun."

"I gotta go talk to my friends for a minute. Then we can go."

I tear myself away from the three of them. That was easy. I only have to walk into a club and I have all the girls I want waiting for me. I don't even have to pick them up anymore. They come to me and pick me up.

I cross the room the rest of the way and meet up with my friends. Jayden Pickett puts his arm around my shoulders and pulls me into their group. "Here he is! The man of the hour."

"Hardly," I tell them. "It looks like I'm just fashionably late."

"You're already working the room, aren't you, you hound?" Wallace Enneman interjects. "Leave some girls for the rest of us."

"I can't help it if you have no game." I tell him. "Trying being as good as this and they might pay attention to you instead."

"Those girls would pay attention to any member of The Billionaires' Club," Rodney Jackman counters. "Girls that young would throw themselves at Dante Helme and he's three times their age."

"Dante is a stud, pure and simple," Wallace replies. "I would totally go out with him if he hadn't gotten married last month."

Jayden turns to me. "Is Dante as much of a stud with the girls as the press makes him out to be?"

I shrug. "He used to be. He's straight now. He doesn't play around with girls since he got together with Emberlynn. They're raising two foster boys. Dante only cares about his family. He wouldn't look sideways at a girl even if she threw herself at him—which they do. Girls still try to tempt him, but he actually seems more disgusted with them when they do. He never gets outright rude, but he makes it clear he isn't interested."

"It must be nice to have so many girls you can actually afford to turn them away," Rodney remarks.

"He doesn't want a different girl every night," Wallace points out. "He already has the one he wants."

"Speaking of which, I gotta go." I pat some of my friends on their shoulders. "It was nice while it lasted, but duty calls."

"Are you really ditching us for those floozies?" Jayden fires back. "I thought we had something real, baby."

The others burst out laughing. "I'll call you later, okay?" I tell him. "Then you and I can spend special time together—just you and me."

The others snort with laughter and elbow him. Jayden joins in the joke. "Enjoy yourself, stud."

"Oh, I will." I turn away and wave to the girls across the dance floor to come and join me.

They meet me in the middle of the floor, put their arms around me, and I put my arms around them on our way to the hallway leading toward the exit.

Lydia starts touching me as soon as we leave the dance floor. Rhianna kisses the side of my neck right behind my ear and then starts nibbling her way around my ear to light me on fire.

Helena slides her hands under my jacket and starts pulling up my shirt to touch my sides and stomach. I'm getting so hard that I can't stand it.

I barely make it halfway down the hall before I turn aside trying to find somewhere I can enjoy these girls right now. I wind up falling against the wall with all three of them stuck to my sides. Lydia stands in front of me rubbing me to raging madness.

I can't stop touching them back. My hand closes on Helena's ass and she moans in high, whining desire in my ear. That sound shoots straight to my nuts.

I creep my hand a little lower to the cleft between her thighs in the back. She arches into my touch and shoves her ass backward to match my speed.

Rhianna crawls her mouth around the front of my neck, starts pulling my tie loose, and giving me big, wet, luscious bites down my chest.

I'm still distracted by both of them when Lydia drops to her knees in front of me, unzips my pants right there, and her hot, powerful mouth closes around my shaft. I can't help but thrust into her mouth.

She doesn't stop until she drains me in gasping release. Holy crap! This is actually happening.

I tear my eyes open and spot the manager's office door standing open on the other side of the hall. He isn't in there at this time of night. He's out on the club floor supervising the bartenders and bouncers and giving instructions to the DJ.

I push myself off the wall and pull all three girls into the manager's office. I have my hands full of all three of them. I don't even take the time to zip myself up. I'll need it out right away anyway.

I shut the door and the girls attack me. Rhianna yanks my belt loose, pushes my pants the rest of the way down, hikes up her skirt, and turns backward to bend over in front of me.

I don't hesitate. I grab her and steer her to the manager's desk so I can push her down on top of it. The other girls start peeling their clothes off, touching each other, kissing me, and stroking me all over my body.

Lydia grabs me by the balls while I slam into Rhianna. Helena lies back on the desk, spreads her legs in front of me, and pulls me face down between her legs even as I pound Rhianna to a screaming frenzy.

Lydia climbs onto the desk next, straddles Helena's face, and starts riding her to the stars. I slip my fingers into Helena's dripping, fragrant channel and pump her to a climax while I'm still taking Rhianna from behind.

The girls scream and throw their heads back in ecstasy. I'm just getting warmed up, but at that moment, the manager walks into the office unawares. He takes one look at us, turns around, and walks straight back out. He knows me, so he knows to make himself scarce.

His presence casts a chill over me. I pull away from the girls, straighten up, and start pulling up my pants. "Let's take this somewhere a little more comfortable and private." I pull Rhianna upright. "Come on. Let's get out of here."

The girls giggle, let out their last sighs, and slither into their dresses. I lead them back out into the hall.

Lydia sucking me helps me calm down, but it doesn't satisfy me. I'm going to take these girls back to my place and enjoy them all night long. The three of them should be enough to wear me out and finally help me settle down—for a little while.

I lead them into the entrance hall, but it's pissing down rain outside. I get on my phone and call my limo driver to come and pick us up. He tells me he's outside, but other traffic at the curb is stopping him from getting any closer to the building.

I tell the girls what's going on. We dash out into the rain, run between some other cars, and I open the rear passenger door so all three of them can get into the limo. I wait until last like the gentleman that I am.

I feel myself getting soaked, but that's just another excuse for the girls to take my clothes off once we get to my apartment. I don't want to catch a cold.

I'm just smiling to myself about that and getting ready to get into the car with them when a taxi comes down the street driving way too fast. I can't tell if the rain interferes with the driver's visibility or what.

It doesn't make a difference why. The vehicle smashes into me, tears the door off the side of the limo, and sends me flying. I slam into another car, fold sideways, and the momentum whips me down hard on the car's trunk.

I barely realize what's happening before an equally powerful force hits me from behind, crushes my whole body under the impact, and I pass out.

Chapter 2: Mila

I peer down into my purse trying to find my ringing phone. I finally get it out, stop in my tracks in the middle of the public library, and tap the screen. I don't recognize the number.

I hold the phone to my ear. "Hello?"

"Hi, Mila," a woman's voice tells me. "This is Laura Rigley. I talked to you yesterday at the grocery store. You invited me to take part in your next photoshoot. I....." She falters. "I want to do it."

"Are you sure?" I ask. "You didn't sound so sure at the store. I don't want to pressure you into something you aren't ready for."

"I'm sure." She takes a deep breath. "I'm sure. I want to do it. Just.....tell me what I have to do."

"When are you available?" I ask. "I can work around your schedule."

"What about tomorrow afternoon—say one o'clock?"

"Yeah, that would be great. Do you want to do it at your place? You can come to my studio if that would make you more comfortable."

"My place would be better. I'm comfortable here—and my husband and kids will be out of the house."

"Okay. I'll see you there."

We hang up. I put my bag under my arm so I can enter her details into my calendar. This is great. I need another model for my latest project. This is working out better than I hoped.

I finish entering the appointment and take my bag out from under my arm to put my phone away. I turn to go on about my business when some random guy comes around a corner and collides with me.

The impact knocks my bag out of my hands. It falls to the floor and a bunch of pictures spill all over the carpet.

The guy calls out, "Sorry!" and hurries away. He doesn't even offer to pick up my stuff.

I groan, roll my eyes, and squat down to pick up the fallen pictures. They're all glossy prints of people's headshots.

I bend over and another pair of hands materializes in front of my eyes. "Let me help you," a man tells me.

I look up and see a young guy leaning over to scoop the pictures together. He's in a wheelchair, but he's young, attractive, and dressed in the most impressive suit I've seen in a long time.

Streaky blonde highlights shoot through his light brown hair. He has blue eyes and his hair cut in a curly-top style that shows off his chiseled features and clear, flawless skin.

The top of him looks muscular and his suit frames his shoulders perfectly inside his jacket. He even wears his tie knotted tightly at his throat with his crisp, white shirt collar standing up straight. This is the nicest I've seen anyone dress to come to the library.

His legs are a different story. They're thin, crooked, fleshless, and twisted inside his pant legs. His polished black leather shoes rest on the footrests. He obviously can't use his legs at all.

His wheelchair sits at a slight angle from the table next to him. A laptop rests on the tabletop. He must have been working on the computer when this happened.

He doesn't notice me watching him. He frowns at the pictures in his hands, turns them around, and shuffles through them to see as many of them as he can. "These are excellent," he murmurs and his eyes shoot up to meet mine. "Are you a professional?"

I blush. "Yeah. These are my bread and butter from all the hopefuls who want to make their name on Broadway." I glance down and take the pictures out of his hands. I accidentally brush his fingers in the process. "Thanks for your help. I'm sorry I disturbed you."

"You didn't disturb me—not at all." He pulls his wheelchair around. He maneuvers it expertly like he's been doing this for a long time. "I'm in the media business. I'm always looking for good photographers. You should let me know if you ever need work. I can give you all the work you want."

I stand up, put the pictures back in my bag, and frown at him. "Is that your way of picking me up?"

He makes a face, takes a business card out of his pocket, and hands it over to me. "You don't have to take my word for it. That number will get you to my assistant, Jeanie. She can refer you to the photography department. You don't ever have to look at me again."

A hint of resentment sneaks into his voice when he says it. I look down at the card. The name at the top is, *Giovanni Nowaczyk, Mammoth Media Group.*

I blink at the card and my eyes dart up to meet his. "You?! You're Giovanni Nowaczyk?!"

He stares straight back up at me with his head pulled back in defensive challenge. "Do you have a problem with that?"

"I just......" I take a second to get my head back into this conversation. "I'm sorry. I just....your work is so impressive. I never thought I would ever get to meet such an icon of the industry. I thought....."

"You thought what? You thought I would be a tall, handsome, impressive hunk?" He snorts and pulls his wheelchair back to his table. "Sorry to disappoint you."

"No, not at all! That isn't what I was thinking at all. I thought you were.....I don't know. I thought you were older—like Yves Saint Laurent or Ralph Lauren. I didn't realize you were so young."

He barely glances at me on the side. "I meant what I said. If you want photography work, I always need people who know what they're doing. I didn't mean it as a pickup line. I wouldn't do that."

He pretends to go back to work on his computer. That must be his way of dismissing me from his awareness.

I think fast. Giovanni Nowaczyk is one of the greatest media presences in the industry. He publishes multiple magazines, periodicals, produces movies, music, video games—everything.

His work is always of the highest quality. My work must be good if he thinks it is.

I take a chance. "If you like my work, maybe you would be interested in participating in another project I'm doing."

He glances up, but only for a second. Then he bends over his computer. "What is it?" he mutters.

"I'm doing a side project. I guess you could call it an art piece. I photograph people's bodies—in a tasteful way."

He snorts again without looking up. "No one wants to see my body," he mutters. "Believe me."

"That's what everyone thinks. See? Everyone has flaws and imperfections that each person thinks makes them ugly and disgusting. This is a way for people to release shame toward their bodies and realize that they're no different from everyone else. The project includes hundreds of people, so it isn't like the viewer is staring at any one particular person. Each person's flaws and imperfections get lost in the crowd."

He turns around and stares at me. "You're serious. You actually want to photograph.....*me?!*"

"Why not? Has anyone seen your body recently?"

"God no!!" he exclaims. "Are you insane? No one wants to see my body."

"I do," I tell him. "Let me photograph you. Some of the people in my show have terrible scars or they're burned badly all over their bodies. You wouldn't be the only person in the show with paralysis or other deformities. Your body is no worse or better than anyone else's. Why don't you try it? The project is totally anonymous." I pull open my bag. "See?"

I hand him a different series of pictures. These are black and white images from my last show.

The pictures show shots of the gallery with hundreds of prints all over the walls. The pictures don't show any of the photographs closely enough for anyone to recognize the models.

All those shots cover the walls. Some of the shots are so high off the ground that no one can see them clearly even if the person was standing right in front of the picture.

His eyes dart from one image to another before he looks away. "It's an interesting idea, but I don't think so."

I put the pictures back in my bag. "If you don't want me to photograph you, you might be interested in a parallel project I'm doing where I interview people about their feelings, relationships, and attitudes toward their bodies—without the photography. I use some of the quotes in the photography show, but your name is never mentioned. No one will ever see your face or know it was you who did the interview."

He shrugs that off and looks away. "Maybe."

I take the hint, mumble, "Thanks again for your help," and walk away.

I just met Giovanni Nowaczyk. That automatically makes today a great day. I've always admired his work.

He's nothing like what I expected. I don't know what I expected, but it isn't that. I wonder why he's so defensive about his body. Maybe something happened to him.

He uses his wheelchair easily and effortlessly. He makes it look like he's been paralyzed all his life or at least for a long time.

I don't know what's going on with him, but it isn't my problem anymore. Meeting him is like meeting a celebrity. He is a celebrity—so why is he working in the public library like a faceless nobody?

I don't understand and I probably never will. I put him out of my mind and keep walking to meet up with my next appointment.

Chapter 3:
Giovanni

I scoot along the seat of my limo just as my driver, Andy, opens the passenger door from outside. He's already taken my wheelchair out of the back, unfolded it, and locked it open on the sidewalk right next to the door.

I pull a long, smooth, polished wooden board from its place in front of the seat. It rests there leaning against the seat under my legs so the board doesn't interfere with anything nor does it lie down flat on the floor.

I pass the board out the door and rest one end on the wheelchair seat and the other end on the limo seat next to me. Then I scoot myself onto the board and across it to the wheelchair.

I remove the board and slide it back inside the limo. I leave it lying on top of the seat this time so I'll be able to get it when I need it to get back into the car.

I push myself up with my arms until I'm sitting comfortably in the wheelchair. I use my hands and arms to position my legs in the right place. I pull my laptop bag out of the car, unlock the wheels, and pull my wheelchair away from the limo so Andy can shut the door.

"Am I picking you up at the same time this afternoon, Sir?" he asks.

"As far as I know. I don't have any appointments or meetings or anything. I'll text you or call you if anything comes up."

"Have a good day, Sir." He heads for the driver's door and shoots me a grin over his shoulder. "Don't let the suckers get you down."

I snort at him. "Thanks, man. You have a good day, too."

He gets in, starts the motor, and drives off into traffic. I spin my chair around and wheel into the Mammoth Media office building across the square.

I brace myself when I get near the automatic sliding entrance doors. This is the first time I've come into the office in weeks. I don't look forward to it.

I roll inside and my worst nightmare comes true before I make it halfway across the lobby. The receptionist at the front desk jumps up, leaves her post, and rushes over to me. "Oh, good morning, Mr. Nowaczyk! Can I help you with anything?"

"You can go back to your desk and do your job, Martina," I mutter out the side of my mouth and burn rubber straight past her to the elevator.

A few other people greet me and they also ask me if I need anything or they give me searching looks when they ask how I'm doing. I try not to be rude, but their obvious concern and attention wears my patience to the breaking point.

A few people outright stare at me when I pull up in front of the elevators. This is why I hardly ever come into the office anymore.

People go out of their way to give me extra space in the elevator. No one comes too near me. They all act like getting hit by a car and getting paralyzed and wheelchair-bound is some kind of contagious disease they can catch by coming near me.

I don't look at anyone. I've been in the building for a total of five minutes and I'm already ready to leave.

I knew this was going to happen. It always happens no matter where I go. Even people I've known for years treat me like I'm either at death's door or they act like I'm a bomb about to go off in their faces.

I ride the elevator up to the fortieth floor, which is where my office is. The rest of the Mammoth executive team also does business up here—each person from his or her own office.

COO Cal Wilberforce stops a conversation midsentence to stare at me. Then he hustles over to walk next to me. He has to keep adjusting his course so he doesn't walk too near me.

"Hey, man! How you doing?" he gushes way too loudly.

"I'm fine, Cal," I mumble. "Everything is spectacular in my world."

"We're having a board meeting this morning, you know," he tells me.

"I know that, Cal," I breathe. "That's what I'm here for."

"Are you.....do we need to do anything to make the boardroom accessible for you?"

"Oh, I don't know. Do you think the floor is flat enough?"

He stops in his tracks and frowns at me before he remembers to hurry after me and catch up. He forces the fakest laugh in history. "That's funny! You haven't lost your sense of humor."

I pull my chair around in my office doorway and face him. "Was there something you wanted, Cal? Do *you* need help with something? Was there something I can do for you?"

He opens his mouth and stops himself. Does he even understand the irony that I'm the one asking him that question everyone else is always asking me?

"Um...." he stammers.

My assistant Jeanie comes up to me right at that moment. "Morning, Mr. Nowaczyk!" she lilts.

"Good morning, Jeanie." I turn my chair around and wheel into the office. I hope that's enough to dismiss Cal from my reality—at least until the board meeting this morning.

Jeanie taps on her tablet. "I've highlighted a bunch of emails in your inbox that are relevant to this morning's meeting. You should probably familiarize yourself with them before they come up on the agenda."

"Thank you, Jeanie," I tell her. "I'll do that."

"I also sent you through the application and resume details of a new photographer who just applied to work for us. I think you'll approve."

My head shoots up when I remember the young woman from the library. I kick myself for not even finding out her name when I had the chance. Maybe I won't need to if she comes to work here.

"Who is it?" I ask. "Is she kind of tall with dark, copper-red hair and glasses?"

"No, this is a man. His name is Tamen Shechter. He used to work for Alvin Blumenthal in the fashion department."

My shoulders slump. Damn. It isn't her. "Okay, thank you, Jeanie. I'll take a look at his portfolio."

She starts to turn away and changes her mind. "Oh, one other thing, Mr. Nowaczyk."

I don't look up from opening my laptop. "What is it, Jeanie?"

"I....um....you know......"

Now I really do look up. "Just tell me if it's something important I need to know for the meeting. I only have an hour and a half to prepare."

"No, it's nothing like that." She turns pink and bursts out in nervous giggles. "It's just...you know.....I'm showing my work at the Nova Gallery. It's my first show and.....I'm opening tonight at eight o'clock.

I....I would really appreciate your support Mr. Nowaczyk. I know you're busy and everything, but......it would really mean a lot to me."

I hesitate. Going out in public is the absolute last thing I want to do. Too many people recognize me. Too many people know about my accident. Too many people want to make a big deal about it and treat me like an invalid even though I'm not one.

Jeanie has been working for me for four years and she's one of the only people in my life who doesn't treat me like that. She doesn't tiptoe around me. She doesn't treat me any differently than she did before the accident. She pretends I'm not paralyzed at all.

"Okay, Jeanie, I'll come," I tell her. "I would really like to see your work. I hope the opening goes well."

She bursts into a huge smile and blushes again. "Thank you so much, Mr. Nowaczyk. I'm a nervous wreck about it. I can't believe I'm actually going to put my pictures on a gallery wall for total strangers to look at!"

I have to smile at her. "I remember how that felt. I'll see you there. Now I better get busy with this. I'll talk to you later."

She grins and blushes again, raises her hand like she wants to wave at me, and leaves me alone. I want to tell her to shut the door, but she doesn't. I don't want to stop work, but I don't want anyone bothering me, either.

I wheel my chair over there so I can shut the door myself. Now I can finally get on with the task at hand. This board meeting is much more important.

Chapter 4: Giovanni

I roll out of the elevator and enter The Billionaires' Club. I'm the only person here who uses the elevator. Everyone else uses the stairs.

Dante Helme bursts into a grin and claps me on the shoulder when I pull into a group with him, Judah Hayes, and Kevin Drake. "Look who's here," Dante exclaims. "Where you been, stranger?"

"I got bitten by a vampire, so I can only come out of my crypt after the sun goes down."

They all laugh. "It's good to see that your vampire blood hasn't affected your razor wit," Judah tells me. "Some of us are going out to dinner in a little while. Jackson is starting a new scholarship fund. Do you want to come with us?"

"Thanks, but I have a prior commitment."

"Who is she?" Kevin asks.

I find myself laughing. "Very funny. My assistant is an aspiring artist. She has a gallery opening tonight, so I'm going to support her."

"Aw!" Dante exclaims. "That's sweet. Good for her for putting herself out there."

"She's really nervous about it and she made it sound like she didn't have many people going, so I thought I better."

"You're a good boss. Hey, did you get that contract I sent over for the new ad campaign?"

"Yeah, I got it. Everything looks good. I'm sure we can accommodate your needs with no problem."

He frowns down at me. None of these guys act like they're talking to a man in a wheelchair. None of them seems to notice that they all have to look down to make eye contact with me.

The guys in The Billionaires' Club have been the best about my accident. They got over it the quickest of everyone in my life. Talking business is way more important to them. They don't give a crap if I'm sitting or standing when they talk to me.

"Do you really think it's good?" Dante asks. "Don't blow sunshine up my ass. Give it to me straight."

"I am giving it to you straight. You know me. I would tell you if I thought it was dog shit."

He laughs. "Yeah, I guess you would."

"Your concepts were on the money. I don't think we'll have to change anything about that. We'll just add the professional images to your existing framework. It should be a piece of cake. Whoever did this really knows their stuff."

He looks away. "I did it."

"You?!" I gasp. "I can't believe it!"

He shrugs that away. "It wasn't that big a deal."

"It was great. I'm stunned."

He squirms, and right then, Jackson Metcalf comes over to us. He goes around the circle shaking hands with everyone, including me. He doesn't see anything different about me since before the accident, either.

He asks all the guys if they're ready to go out to dinner. "Do you want to come with us, champ?" he asks me. "You're more than welcome. We were planning to go to the Crow's Nest, but we can change it to the Russia House if you come. I don't suppose it matters where we go."

"Don't change your plans. I have to be somewhere. I'll catch up with you fellas later."

They all head for the stairs. I have no more reason to stick around, so I ride the elevator down to the ground floor. I meet up with all of them outside the building. They get into Dante's limo and I get into mine.

Andy drives me down to Tribeca for Jeanie's opening. I cringe when I get out of the car and see Rhianna and Lydia inside. They're hobnobbing with a couple of other guys in suits.

The girls both spot me through the gallery's front windows and immediately look away. It's always like this.

I take a few deep breaths and brace myself before I go in there. I'm doing this for Jeanie. I'm not here to socialize or pick up girls or anything else. I just have to make a polite appearance. Then I can leave.

I roll up to the entrance. Some of the other gallery patrons see me coming and open the door for me to enter. I could do it myself, but I've learned not to make a big deal about it.

I thank them as politely as I can and try to make my way through the crowd. It's kind of impossible because there are so many people already in here.

I wouldn't be able to move at all, but people have the same exaggerated reaction to my presence. They leap out of my way, gush on and on excusing themselves, and a few people ask me if they can help me with anything.

I answer as politely as I can that I'm fine. I look around and spot Jeanie on the other side of the room.

She practically pisses herself when I pull up in front of her. She actually dives for me and hugs me. Then she fans her hand in front of her face. "Oh, my gosh! I can't believe I'm actually here!" she pants. "This is the craziest thing I've ever done!"

"It isn't crazy at all," I tell her. "Congratulations. I'm proud of you for pursuing your passion and putting it out there. You deserve this."

She bursts out in nervous laughter, but she has to stop and shake hands with a few people just then. She gets distracted, so that leaves me mercifully on my own.

I take a look at the pictures behind her. Her work covers one side of the gallery. Other artists are showing in other areas of the building.

Her work is all bland, boring, underdeveloped landscapes with no soul, no message, and absolutely nothing to distinguish them. They aren't complex enough even for me to call them art. They're really just paintings.

I wheel down the wall and study each one taking in the whole aesthetic. I'm probably the worst person she could possibly invite to her opening. I know too much about art.

I would never tell her what I really think, though. I want to encourage her. She'll develop in time—or she won't. She's too valuable to me. I would never criticize her work or make her think she isn't good enough.

I am proud of her for having the courage to show in public. That means something.

I stop at the end of the wall where it meets up with the next wall running perpendicular to this one. I stare at dozens and dozens of black and white photographs of people posing naked for the camera.

I recognize these pictures instantly. They're the same photographs the woman from the library showed me.

Her work covers five walls of the gallery. The pictures spill around corners and rise ten feet off the ground.

I see now that she's right. There are so many of these pictures that they make the subjects totally anonymous. I can wheel my chair right up to them and look straight at each person's face, but I would never recognize any of these people if I saw them in public.

One of the women is terribly burned over her whole head and half her body. The rest of her looks normal. Her one normal breast, her stomach, hips, and legs lie exposed to the camera.

She even sits with her legs apart so I can see all her genitals exposed. The picture somehow humanizes her. There's nothing sexual about the pose. She's just a normal woman who happens to be burned.

Another guy looks like an absolute stud. He's tall, strong, muscular, and he stands in a bodybuilding pose with both arms raised to flex his biceps for the camera. He's also naked. All the subjects are.

Any guy would be proud to look like him, but one of his legs is withered, deformed, and as skeletal as mine. That one leg doesn't look like it belongs to the rest of him.

Each person has some flaw, blemish, scar, or deformity that mars their perfection. Some of these people are morbidly obese or fatally malnourished.

Some are old, wrinkled, and covered in sagging skin. One of the women is missing one breast with a hideous scar covering half her chest. Another man is missing both legs and one of the women sits in front of the camera with a gaping hole where one eye should be.

Each person stands or sits in front of the camera with everything hanging out for the world to see—and yet these photographs somehow make these people look so unbelievably beautiful.

I inch my chair down the wall taking in one picture after another. Each one is a magnificent work of art in its own right. Each picture calls up so many hidden questions about our bodies, our lives, and the shame that makes us keep all of this hidden.

She's right. This is the best possible antidote to that shame. I see now that each of these people is as perfect as Michelangelo's David. Their scars and deformities don't make these people any less beautiful.

I could never do anything like this. I could never let anyone take a picture of my body. No way in hell.

I come to the end of the wall and stop my chair there. I feel myself shaking with a mixture of emotions. This show.....it affects me in ways I've never imagined anything could.

I find myself staring at the label next to one of the pictures. It lists the subject's name and the photographer's name. Mila Knapp. That's her. That's the woman I met in the library.

She's printed out quotes from her interviews. Small plaques scatter between the photographs. Each plaque gives the words each person said in their interview about their relationship with their body.

One plaque reads, *My body is my worst enemy.*

The next says, *I feel like a normal person trapped in a giant, amorphous blob. I feel like an alien has eaten me and I'm trapped inside its stomach where I can't get out.*

Another reads, *I don't have any mirrors in my house because I can't stand to look at myself, not even from the neck up.*

People stare at me or look away when I go out in public, another reads. *I hardly ever go out because I can't deal with their reactions.*

I turn my chair around and start wheeling back in the other direction. I notice new pictures, new people, and whole new dimensions of reality on my way back to the other end of the room.

I don't know what this means, but it means something—something big. I can't ignore this.

Chapter 5: Giovanni

I turn outward to face the art gallery once I make my second pass down Mila Knapp's wall of pictures. I can't bring myself to go check out the other four walls of photographs. She must have five hundred pictures in this gallery alone.

This is massive—and I don't mean the number of pictures. It's almost like she's capturing a fundamental reality of what it means to be human.

This is the human race right here. She's documenting the private hell we all live in with this shame that our bodies aren't good enough. What if she's right? What if I'm no different from all these other people?

I *am* not different from them. I have something wrong with my body. I'm still human. I'm still the same species as all of them. I already knew that, but this show makes it all so much painfully clearer.

I don't know what to think. I turn my chair away and someone switches the volume back on. I hear people nearby talking about Mila's work.

"She's so talented, sensitive, and insightful," one man gushes. "You wouldn't think nude photographs could communicate so much. It's.....it's breathtaking."

Another woman wipes away tears. "Posing for her was the best thing that's ever happened to me! I thought my life was over—but after seeing her work—everything changed for me. The clouds parted and the sun came out for the first time in years—ever since the accident happened."

I don't let myself see the people talking. I don't want to see their faces in case I've just been sitting here looking at their naked bodies.

Someone bumps into my chair right then and says, "Oh, excuse me!" I glance up to reassure the person. It's no one I recognize. It might be someone from Mila's display. How would I know? I would never recognize any of those people in real life.

I forget not to look around. I see the woman wiping away tears. I don't recognize her, either. I can't tell who in this room might be one of her subjects. They could be anyone. Any random person I meet on the street might be one of her subjects. I would never know.

I wouldn't know what secret scars they keep hidden under their clothes. I wouldn't know their stories or their private shame. We all work so hard to keep it hidden from each other. Why?

I do the same thing. I haven't let anyone see my body since the accident. I'm ashamed of it. I don't even let myself use home help or hire an aide to help me do things. I want to pretend the accident never happened and that my life is exactly the same as it was before.

Jeanie comes over to me and thanks me again for coming. I tell her again that I'm proud of her and she has a great art career in front of her. She won't stop blushing and laughing.

I'm just about to make my excuses to leave when I see Mila across the gallery. She's one of the only people here wearing casual clothes.

She wears tight brown slacks, a short leather blazer pinched at the waist, high-heeled ankle boots, and a dark purple blouse with big, pointed lapels.

Her long, bouncy, wavy copper-red hair tumbles from a high half-ponytail with wisps of hair curling around her face, ears, and neck. Thin-rimmed glasses perch on her nose and give her a bookish, intellectual look.

She's stunning, but in a completely different way from all the club crawlers that used to throw themselves at me every night. I wouldn't have looked sideways at Mila before.

I barely notice that Rhianna and Lydia are still in the gallery working the room. They completely ignore me. They don't even say hello to me or look in my direction a second time.

Mila is in the middle of a conversation with an older, grey-haired man in a suit. She nods at something he says and uses her forefinger to move a lock of hair out of her eyes.

She balances a tiny saucer in one hand and holds the handle of a small espresso mug in the other. She's so engrossed in the conversation that she doesn't see or notice anything else.

She stands on the opposite side of the gallery from her own work. She isn't holding court or answering questions or greeting all her admiring fans. She looks like she was checking out some other artist's work when this man started talking to her.

I can't leave without talking to her. I don't know why I feel so drawn to her. I understand her work so much better, now that I've seen it. She didn't do it justice when she described it in the library. Not even seeing photographs of the gallery did her work justice.

She's gorgeous, talented, sensitive, and creative, but I don't want to talk to her to pick her up. I know better than to suggest that. I just want to talk to her.

Some part of me wants to crawl inside her mind and figure out how she works. I want to find out what made her come up with the idea for this project. It's so simple and yet such a stroke of artistic genius.

It takes me a while to work my way through the crowd. I don't have to ask anyone to move. They all figure it out for themselves soon enough.

She finishes her conversation just as I come through the crowd to meet up with her. She smiles at the guy, shakes his hand, and they both nod before she turns around.

She stops dead in her tracks when she sees me. I hold out my hand. "Mila Knapp?" I ask. "We meet again."

She snaps out of it immediately and shakes my hand. "Good to see you. I hope you didn't come here to see my show."

"I didn't. I had no idea who you were and I had no idea you were showing at this gallery—but I would have come if I had known. Your display is amazing. I'm impressed."

She doesn't hear that. She frowns at me. "Why are you here, then?"

"Jeanie Vanderkamp is my assistant. She's opening tonight. I'm here to support her."

Mila's expression clears and she nods. "That was nice of you."

"I'm curious about this project of yours....."

"I'm calling it the Infection Project," she tells me. "The name comes from one of the quotes. One of the subjects said he felt like his shame was an infection eating him away from the inside. He said he felt like the shame infection was what made his body mutate into something that wasn't human."

I nod. "That's a good name. So what made you decide to do all of this?"

She shrugs. "I saw a need for it. I saw a lot of people suffering with the same shame paralysis—kind of like you when you said no one wants to see your body."

I look away.

"Have you thought at all about taking part in the project?" she asks. "You could just do the interview. Some people get value out of just talking about their situations—and it helps other people to hear and read the reactions and feelings of others."

I glance up at her. She stares straight back down into my eyes. She's one of the very few who doesn't shy away from looking at me.

She doesn't shy away from talking to me about any of this, either. She's the first person who has done that. Most people avoid the subject entirely.

Seeing, reading, and hearing others who are going through the same thing helps me, too. She's right about that. Her show really does help me feel better about my situation.

I didn't realize I had a problem with it, but I must. I'm still not ready to let anyone see me with my clothes off.

"All right," I tell her. "I'll do the interview."

She bursts into a brilliant smile. "Wonderful. Thank you. I'm really grateful. I wouldn't be able to do this project without people like you having the courage to talk about it."

"So.....what do we have to do? Do we meet at the library?"

"It's a little too public." She glances down at my chair. "I would normally invite the person to my studio, but unfortunately, it isn't wheelchair accessible."

"Why don't you come to my apartment? When do you want to do it?"

"My schedule is flexible, so I can work around whenever is convenient for you. I also ask people if I can voice record the interview.

That way I don't have to sit there typing the whole time to save your answers. We can just talk normally and I can go back over your responses later in case I forget anything."

"That sounds fine." I turn around in my chair and take a notebook and pen out of the backpack hanging behind my seat.

I become aware of her watching the way my body moves under my suit. She pays much closer attention to me than I'm used to from anyone else.

I scribble down my address. "I have business meetings all day to-morrow, so why don't we do it Thursday morning? How long does the interview take?"

"That just depends on how long our conversation lasts. Some only last half an hour. Others can go for hours if the person has a lot to get off their chest."

I find myself laughing. I hand over the piece of paper and put my notebook and pen away. "We should probably start the interview in the morning, then. How about ten o'clock? Does that work for you?"

"That's perfect." She lowers her eyes to the sheet in her hand. "Thank you for doing this. I'm really grateful."

"You don't have to keep saying that. Your work is truly impressive. I want to support it if I can. I'll see you Thursday."

I shake her hand one more time, pull my chair away, and wheel outside. I might live to regret this, but she did say the interview was totally anonymous. She might not even use my comments in her show.

No one will ever find out that I'm the one who said it if she does use it. My words will blend in with everyone else's quotes on that wall. I'll become invisible—which is exactly what I want to be.

Chapter 6: Mila

I climb the stairs to leave the subway and glance up at huge high-rise buildings all around me. I check my phone, read the address on the piece of paper in my hand, and compare it to my phone again.

The address is right, but the building is an office tower, not an apartment building.

I don't know why I thought Giovanni Nowaczyk would live in a normal apartment building. His apartment is probably a giant penthouse with its own pool and everything. He can certainly afford it.

I've been doing research on him ever since I met him at the gallery. He's one of the youngest members of The Billionaires' Club and he has a reputation for being a ladies' man—and not in a good way.

No one can say anything bad about his professional reputation, though. His media company produces only the highest quality material. Every other big business company in the country and even the world wants him to do their next ad campaign.

He's produced dozens of movies that have won multiple awards. He runs record labels with chart-topping musicians on his books. Everything he touches works out to be the best in the business—whatever branch of the media and entertainment industry he works in.

I walk into the office building lobby and approach the reception desk. A young Asian woman smiles at me from behind her computer. "Can I help you with anything today, Ma'am?" she asks.

"I'm Mila Knapp," I tell her. "I have an appointment to see Giovanni Nowaczyk."

She only smiles. "Yes, Ma'am. He's expecting you. You can go on up. He's on the forty-ninth floor."

I don't ask which apartment he's in. His apartment might cover the entire floor for all know.

I get into the elevator with a bunch of people in suits. They all look like they're at work. A few of them discuss meetings, schedules, projects, timeframes, and budgets. No one here acts like they're in the lower levels of an apartment building.

The other people in the elevator all get out on the lower floors. I'm eventually the only person in here. The elevator keeps going up and up. It doesn't stop on any other floors and no other people get on.

My heart starts racing the closer I get to meeting Giovanni again. He doesn't act like a billionaire or a celebrity. I wouldn't have expected someone as rich, famous, talented, and savvy as he is to act so casual and even humble.

His reputation paints him as an arrogant hothead. A few people have even made public comments that they wouldn't do business with him at all if his company wasn't so influential and his work wasn't so good.

He doesn't act that way at all—not around me.

The media reports also state that he only became paralyzed two years ago when he got run over by a car. Maybe that had something to do with toning him down.

The elevator dings and I jump out of my skin. The noise sounds extra loud in the silence. The doors open and I step out into a carpeted hallway with doors on either side. I don't know which of these doors leads to Giovanni's apartment.

I'm standing there trying to figure it out when he comes to one of them and opens it from the inside. He steers his wheelchair with one hand and opens the door with the other.

He answers the door wearing a suit this time, too—everything except the jacket. He looks just as put together in a clean white business shirt and dark navy-blue tie and pants. He dresses like this is a business meeting.

His eyes flash when he looks down the hall at me. "Down here," he calls.

I walk over there. "Thanks. This place is like a maze."

"It is, really." He pulls his chair aside so I can walk into his apartment. "I just moved in here recently, so I'm still learning my way around."

He shuts the door behind me. I enter a big penthouse suite as lavish as I expected it to be, but it's obviously been built for someone in a wheelchair. A ramp drops from the entrance hall to a big, open-plan living room and kitchen.

This place has been designed with extra space around all the furniture. It doesn't quite look the way an ordinary apartment would. Everything about this penthouse feels just different enough to be noticeable.

The kitchen counter is much lower. None of the counters or sinks come up past my thighs. The fridge is half the height of a normal fridge, too, so Giovanni can reach everything from his chair.

Large sections of the countertops don't have cabinets underneath them so he can pull his chair right in underneath them without bumping into anything. I walk around checking everything out.

"This is so cool!" I exclaim. "I've actually never been a wheelchair-accessible apartment before. This is like going to the zoo or something."

He snorts with laughter. "At least you have the tact to say so out loud. I only moved in here after the accident. My other place wasn't accessible, so I had to move. Hardly anything is accessible. You would be surprised."

"I bet." I put my handbag on the floor next to one of the living room couches. They look the same as any ordinary couch.

Enormous glass panel windows open onto the terrace outside. Everything about the flooring and flagstone pavement outside is perfectly flat and smooth so he doesn't have to drive over anything in his wheelchair. Even the door track is flat.

An enormous pool covers part of the terrace. Part of the pool has been sectioned off into a lane so someone can swim laps if they want to.

Giovanni wheels his chair into the living room and watches me explore his apartment. "This place is awesome," I exclaim. "It actually looks like a billionaire lives here."

"No billionaires live here." He brakes his wheelchair next to one of the couches. "How do you want to do this?"

I turn around, grab my purse, and sit on the couch opposite him. "Are you still okay with me recording our interview?"

"Sure. Do you need to hook me up to a lie detector machine or anything like that?"

I laugh. "Do you really plan to lie about any it?"

"I don't know. That depends on the questions you ask."

I try not to smirk when I see the way he's looking at me. I don't want to let myself think he may have invited me here to because he thinks of me in that way.

I take my phone out of my purse and a notebook and pen. He watches everything I do with a hawkish, evaluating air. I feel like I'm the one getting interviewed here.

Chapter 7: Mila

I switch on the voice recorder and put my phone on the coffee table between me and Giovanni. He stays in his chair. I guess moving to the couch would be too much trouble—and it isn't like he isn't already sitting down.

"So how would you like to start?" I ask.

"Don't you already know that? Don't you have a set of preprepared questions?"

"Not really. I just kind of wing it and let the person talk. Why don't you start by telling me how your life has changed since your accident?"

He stares at me and snorts again. "You're joking, right? You can see how my life has changed since my accident. I'm in a wheelchair."

"I don't mean all of that. I'm not talking about all the logistical stuff like how you get stuff out of the refrigerator. I'm talking about you. I'm talking about your relationship with yourself and your body. How has that changed since the accident?"

He snorts again and looks away. He doesn't answer immediately.

I don't prompt him. He remains silent for a long time and refuses to turn his head or look at me. I've done enough of these interviews to recognize when my questions make the interviewee uncomfortable.

He finally jerks around, levels me with a hard look, and growls under his breath. "I guess you could say my relationship with myself and my body changed after the accident."

"How did it change?"

"Do you know the episode of *Seinfeld* where George's mother catches him jacking off in the bathroom, goes off on him, and says he's treating his body like an amusement park?"

I burst out laughing. "I'm sorry. I can't help it. I don't mean to make light of your circumstances."

He waits for me to pull myself together before he goes on. "I guess that's how I thought of my body before the accident. I thought it was great. I thought it was fun and enjoyable and healthy. I thought I was awesome."

"And how do you think of it now?"

"Now I think of it like one of those giant robotic suits from *Pacific Rim*. I think of my body as a Terminator robot and I'm the driver. I drive it around and get it to do what I want it to do."

"Why did you say that no one would want to see your body if I photographed you?" I ask.

He scoffs in my face. "No one would."

"But why?"

He makes a face. "Isn't it obvious?"

"No, it isn't." I look down at his legs. "What's wrong with you?"

"I'm paralyzed! Can't you see that? I can't walk."

"So? Anyway, we aren't talking about that. Why do you think no one would want to see your body?"

"For a start because I'm covered in scars from the waist down. The car that hit me crushed my legs and pelvis. I had to go through a bunch of surgeries and my legs aren't the right shape anymore."

"And how does that make you feel?"

"It isn't how it makes me feel. I wouldn't care at all."

"Are you sure about that? It seems like you care about it a lot."

"I don't give a crap what I look like. It's everyone else in the world who cares so much."

I frown at him. "Who cares so much about what you look like?"

"Well....girls for a start."

"Oh, I see. So girls treat you differently?"

"Of course they do. They used to throw themselves at me the minute I walked into a place. Now they won't even look at me. Girls that I went out with or hooked up with who used to rub themselves all over me—now they pretend I don't exist. They don't even say hello to me."

"And how does that make you feel?"

"It pisses me off, if you want to know the truth. I know they only threw themselves at me and fooled around with me because I'm some bigshot billionaire or something like that and they probably thought some of that would rub off on them if they just banged me a few times."

"How does that feel—knowing they were only interested in you for that?"

"I don't care about it—and I never cared about them. I guess that's what I'm saying. I never cared about it while it was happening."

"Did that change after the accident? Did you start caring that they don't even look at you and won't even greet you just because you're in a wheelchair?"

"I don't care about that. It's everyone else that rubs me raw."

"What does everyone else do?"

"They act like I'm made of glass. They act like they have to flutter around me and fan my brow and cater to my every whim. They don't treat me like a person. They treat me like I'm a disaster waiting to happen or like I'm a disaster that already has happened. People I've been doing business with for years won't shut the hell up about what they can do for me and asking me if I'm okay and if they need to modify the boardroom to make it accessible."

"Are they just trying to be considerate? Wouldn't the boardroom need to be accessible?"

"I might be able to believe that if people didn't drop everything they were doing the minute I enter a room and go into a fit of hysterics acting like I'm about to collapse with a fatal heart attack or whatever it is they're worried about. I can count on one hand the number of people who treat me like a normal human being who just happens to be in a wheelchair. They act like I'm about to die right in front of them when I'm healthier than all of them put together."

"Maybe they just haven't gotten used to it," I suggest. "Maybe it's just new to them and they'll get used to it in time."

"They better hurry up and get used to it," he snarls. "I have to live with it. They can, too."

I lean back on the couch. Now we're getting somewhere. He gets more agitated and his voice rises as he lets out his frustrations.

"I did some research on you and saw some pictures of you from before the accident," I tell him. "You seem to have done a lot to improve your fitness since it happened."

"I have to," he tells me. "I have to use my upper body strength to move myself around. I have to get into and out of my car. I have to get into and out of the shower. That's what I mean about treating my body like an amusement park. I guess I thought my body was more of a chick magnet before. That's about all I thought it was good for—that and enjoying good food, good drink, and good women."

I find myself smiling at him. I really wish my cheeks weren't flushing so much. "You don't see yourself as a chick magnet now?"

"I'm not a chick magnet now. No woman would want to live with this."

I frown at him. "Why not?"

"Please," he sneers. "No woman is ever going to want to get with me ever again. I can concentrate on being as healthy as possible so I can keep living my life. All of that is off the table for me from now on."

"I don't understand what you mean." I find myself looking down at his body. "Are you still sexually functional?"

"Yes, I am. I have nerve damage in my legs. That's what makes me paralyzed. The rest of me works just fine."

"Then what makes you think a woman wouldn't want to get together with you? Women get together with paraplegics who *aren't* sexual function."

He flinches and looks away. "No one would ever want to have anything to do with this body," he growls. "It's disgusting. No one sees me as a sexual being because I'm not one."

"Why would you say that about yourself when you obviously still are one? Don't you ever get frustrated that you don't have a sex life anymore?"

He spins around fast and actually yells at me. "Of course I do! What do you think I am—some kind of animal or robot that can just turn off how I feel? Don't you think I want it the same way I always did? It's driving me crazy! I would have to pay some prostitute to fuck me—and even then she wouldn't be able to hide that I disgust her. Do you think I like being a freak no one wants to touch? How would you feel if you were me? No one would want to live like this. You sure wouldn't. You can have any guy you want."

I shrug that away. "I might want it. You're attractive, healthy, intelligent, driven, and articulate. You're everything I would look for in a guy, but it would be what's in your heart that would make me love you. You being in a wheelchair wouldn't stop me."

He looks away again and lowers his voice to a broken murmur. "It isn't just that."

"What is it, then? Is it because you're scarred? Scars can be beautiful. They show what a person is on the inside. I wouldn't want to be with anyone who didn't have scars."

"I don't see you displaying pictures of your naked body for everyone to see," he counters.

"Yes, I do. I'm in the Infection show."

He spins around and gasps. "You are? Where? I didn't see you."

"The whole point of the show is for people to blend in the crowd—to show that we're all the same in that way. I'm no different from everyone else. I have my own flaws. Everyone does. Even celebrity supermodels have them. They just cover it up with makeup and a whole lot of airbrushing."

He yanks the brakes off his wheels, pulls his chair away, and rolls over to the big glass windows looking out at the pool. "I wouldn't want to get together with you anyway," he mutters under his breath.

"Is that because I put myself on show?"

"No, not at all," he murmurs. "I wouldn't want to disrespect you the way I've disrespected so many other girls. I kick myself for the way I acted before. I'm a lot more ashamed of that than what my body looks like—especially now when it's so obvious that none of them ever gave a shit about me. I never gave a shit about any of them, either. That's the worst part. I have no reason to get all hurt and shit that they don't want to have anything to do with me. I knew at the time that it was totally superficial. It was just as superficial for me—so why should I care?" He passes his hand across his eyes. "It's embarrassing. I acted like a child running wild in a candy store. I understand now why the other guys at the club never took me seriously. It's a miracle they even still respect me at all. I don't."

I don't know what to say, so I don't say anything at all. I didn't expect him to open up this much.

He finally turns his chair around and wheels it back over to the couches. "Do you have any other questions for me?" he asks.

"Not unless you want to keep talking. We can keep talking as long as you want to. Most people I interview have a lot to talk about. Most of them have never talked to anyone about how they feel or how their lives have really changed because of their circumstances. I'm happy to listen if you want to keep talking."

"I have a question for you, Mila," he tells me.

My head shoots up. "You do? What do you want to know?"

"I would like you to go out to dinner with me."

I blink at him. "Are you serious?"

"Yes, absolutely. I respect the work you're doing and I admire you for it. I didn't get it when you told me about it at the library. I didn't understand until I saw the show for myself. Go out to dinner with me—totally obligation-free. I like talking to you, but I'd like the opportunity to do it when you weren't interviewing me for your project. This would just be a social get-together—nothing official."

I take a second to fully understand what he's asking. He did just say he wouldn't want to get together with me—not in that way. Maybe he's telling the truth. Maybe he just wants to have dinner and talk—as acquaintances.

"Okay," I tell him. "That would be nice."

He rolls forward and holds out his hand to shake mine. "How about eight o'clock on Saturday? Are you busy then? Do you have to go to the gallery?"

"I don't have to go anywhere. I only went to the gallery that night to support Jeanie."

He looks up. "Do you know her?"

"Sure. All the artists who show at the Nova know each other. We all talk and support each other's work. It's really helpful to talk to other people who are doing the same thing."

"But aren't you....you know....in competition with each other?"

"We don't see it that way. We just focus on doing our best work and helping each other on the journey."

"Okay. That's an interesting way of putting it. I didn't realize Jeanie had a whole community of other artists she was working with on the side."

"You said she's your assistant. How much do you know about her personal life?"

"I thought I knew a lot about it. Maybe I was wrong."

I switch off the voice recorder on my phone, put the phone away, and stand up. "I really appreciate you doing this—and I know the audience really appreciates it. Your contribution is helping other people get over this shame infection, too."

He holds my hand extra long when he shakes it. His eyes burn up at me from his chair. "You're the one who is helping people, Mila. You helped me a lot with this show—and by listening. I'm grateful for that."

I smile at him and wind up blushing. I shouldn't. "I'll see you Saturday."

He lets me out of the apartment and I ride the elevator all the way back down to the lobby. That interview went so much better than I ever expected.

He's interesting. He has so much going for him, but the accident obviously left him scarred in other ways that go deeper than his body.

I hope my work can help him. He deserves to put that pain behind him and realize just how much he has going for him.

Chapter 8: Giovanni

I wheel my chair up to the front of Mila's apartment building and stop at the bottom of the steps. This is another inaccessible impasse I can't get over.

I compress my lips, pull out my phone, and call her. "I was trying to be all dashing and everything by coming to your door, but this building has too many stairs. I'm outside. I'm sorry, but you have to come down and meet me here."

"I'm on my way," she tells me and hangs up.

I pull my chair back from the stairs and wait for her. People pass me on the sidewalk and stare back and forth between me and the limo. Andy stands there waiting, too. I can think of a few slightly less awkward ways to start a date.

I don't let myself think I'm taking Mila on a date. I told her I wasn't interested in her, but I really, secretly am. She said me being in a wheelchair wouldn't stop her. She also implied that me being scarred wouldn't stop her, either. Do I dare to believe I have a chance?

I don't want to get my hopes up. I have to be cautiously realistic.

The girls I associated with before aren't much of a standard to live up to, but who's to say Mila won't reject me the way they do?

She doesn't act the way they do. She doesn't ignore me. She doesn't act like me being paralyzed is a problem at all. That's the way I feel, but the rest of the world hasn't gotten the memo yet.

She finally comes out of the building. I'm relieved to see that she isn't dressed for a date—not a big, fancy, billionaire-style date. She wears a different pair of close-fitting capri pants that show off her figure, a different blazer, and a pale-yellow blouse this time.

Everything else about her looks the same. She takes one look at my suit and bursts into a grin. "Do you take your suit off when you shower and go to bed?"

"Never," I tease. "I'm hoping it permanently fuses to my body. Then I won't ever have to change my clothes."

I escort her back to the limo. She slides into the seat. I take the board out from its place, put it across the seat, and slide over there to sit next to her.

She watches everything in wide-eyed fascination until I put the board away and Andy folds up my chair to put it into the trunk.

"Wow!" she breathes. "That is so smart!"

"It was either that or start driving around in a mini-van and I definitely was NOT going to do that. I didn't want to give up the finer things just because some cab driver lost control of his vehicle."

"It's really an inventive way to get into and out of a car." She settles back on the seat. Andy shuts the door and pulls out into traffic. "So what's tonight's topic of conversation?"

"I'm curious about you. Was it hard for you to find people who wanted to be subjects for the Infection show? It must have taken more to convince them when you had fewer pictures. Everyone's identity would have been a lot more visible."

"It wasn't, really. I started out by photographing people privately. I didn't plan to show the pictures. I just wanted to use it as a way to help people accept what they saw as their own imperfections. I already had about two hundred prints by the time I did my first show. It keeps snowballing and getting bigger, but it's always been pretty anonymous even in the early days—ever since the show went public. It's a lot easier to get models now."

"How long do you think you'll keep it going?" I ask. "It must end at some point, won't it?"

"I don't know. I keep adding to it. Marlena, the gallery owner, just wants to keep showing it for as long as people keep coming in and looking at it."

"None of the pictures are for sale, are they?" I ask. "I can't imagine anyone giving permission for that."

"No, of course not—and the entire show isn't for sale, either. That's one of the stipulations I offer when I photograph some-one—that I'll never sell the pictures either individually or as a group. We sign a contract beforehand so the person knows they're protected."

"That's a good idea."

"What about you?" she asks. "How did you get into media?"

"I started as a photographer. I started when I was about twelve and I got a job when I was seventeen. I started as an intern at a fashion magazine, but I hated their aesthetic. I started copying some of their style shots, but I put my own spin on them and showed how I would do it differently if I had been in charge of running the magazine. I made the mistake of posting some of the pictures on social media and I got fired for criticizing the company."

She laughs. "Woops."

"Anyway, the artistic director of a different company saw my work and liked it. He offered me a job as a layout designer and it all spiraled from there. I did a few side projects on my own that got noticed and

I used the money to buy out the first magazine I worked for. That's how it started."

She cocks her head to study me. She studies me much more closely than anyone else does. No one ever looks at me like this, not even my friends.

"Do you ever miss the creative side of doing your own work?" she asks. "Don't you miss being a photographer?"

"My work is creative. I can express myself creatively on a much bigger scale now because I have a much bigger canvas to work with."

She faces front. "I guess so."

The limo pulls up in front of the restaurant just then. We get out in reverse order. Mila watches me slide across the board to my wheelchair. Then she gets out and we walk into the lobby of the nearest building.

We get into the elevator and ride up to the second floor. We walk into a giant restaurant with a big open hot line in the middle of the room. All the chefs work over open flames inside a rectangular counter facing every side of the room.

Mila beams at me when we sit down at the table. The concierge takes the chair away from my place. "This is so cool!" she exclaims.

I really want to take her hand and draw her attention back to me. I want to make this into a real date, but I'm not ready to go there.

One of the chefs turns something on the grill and a jet of flame shoots into the air. Some of the patrons exclaim and gasp out in excited amazement.

Mila shoots me a grin on the side and turns around to face me. The expression on her face gives me a wild thrill. This is the first time any woman has paid any attention to me since the accident.

In fact, this is the first time any woman has paid any attention to me ever. I realize that now. The women I messed around with before—they didn't even see me. I didn't exist to them. They treated me as much like a piece of meat as I treated them.

This is the first time I've actually sat across the table from a woman and had dinner with her like we might actually be interested in each other.

That's the problem with becoming successful at such a young age. Women aren't interested in anything else. No one sees the person that I am—or they didn't. They only cared about my money and the bragging rights of telling their friends they hooked up with me.

I am interested in Mila. That's what's so different about this. I don't even really care about hooking up with her. I just want to spend time with her and get to know her.

I'm not sure how I feel about hooking up with anyone. I would have to trust someone a lot before I went that far. It would take a lot to convince me that the woman wasn't going to treat my body like something they accidentally stepped in on the sidewalk.

She's the first and only person who has ever given me the impression that she wouldn't mind what I look like. She's the first and only person who seems to care a lot more about the person that I am.

She said that in the interview, but all the rest of her behavior says the same thing so much more eloquently. I would have dismissed it otherwise.

She says it's what's in my heart that would make her love me.

Thinking that makes me ache to prove myself to her. I want her to love me. That's the truth. She's the first and only woman I've ever felt that way about. I want to be worthy of her—and I'm not now—not when I've been such a player.

I put all of that on the back burner and just concentrate on having a nice evening with her. The waitress comes and Mila and I both order.

"How are the headshots working out in terms of paying your bills?" I ask. "I meant what I said. You should apply at Mammoth if you need a job."

Her smile slips. "Is that why you asked me out—to recruit me?"

"Of course not. I'm just saying. You aren't making any money on the Infection show. How else are you going to keep a roof over your head?"

She shrugs. "I don't mind doing the headshots. It's a living—and I always get a steady supply of people who want them. Satisfied customers tell their friends where they got theirs and I get a lot of referrals."

"Do you do any other media—like graphic design or anything like that?"

"Naw. I don't want to. I've only ever been interested in photography. I never wanted to do anything else."

"You're very good."

"You keep saying that. I bet you were pretty good, too. You must have been if you got noticed and offered such a good job."

I shrug that away. "I was pretty good, but I'm better at this. I'm better as the conductor of the whole orchestra."

She laughs. "I can just see you sitting there like a spider at the center of your web plucking the strings and making things happen all around you."

I can't help but smile at her. I like making her laugh. She's the only person I can talk to like this. I can't even talk to the guys at the club like this. She opens up a whole new world of possibilities.

Chapter 9: Giovanni

Mila and I come out of the restaurant. She glances around. "Where's your short bus?"

I burst out laughing. "Hush your mouth, girl."

She beams at me. "I really don't blame you for not wanting to drive a minivan. That would have been the ultimate humiliation."

"Come take a walk with me." I turn my chair away. "I don't want to take you home yet and it was so noisy in the restaurant."

I head down the sidewalk to the crosswalk and push the button to activate the signal. We wait for the green flashing walking indicator and cross to the pier on the other side.

"Is this what you call walking?" she asks. "What do you call it when you walk with your arms?"

I laugh. She makes me happy. I love that she can joke about my disability without it being insulting.

"Let's call it, 'stalking'," I tell her.

Now it's her turn to laugh. "So you're stalking me now? Great."

"Do you have any ideas for other projects you want to do?" I ask.

"I have a few, but they're more in the embryonic stages. I'm not ready to do anything about them until I develop more of a concept of what I want to do and why. I guess that was the whole point of the Infection show. I had a clear idea of what I wanted to accomplish and the message I wanted it to convey. That part of it was never in any doubt."

"The message definitely comes across. It was....moving."

She smiles down at me. "I'm glad you got that. Seeing the way it affects people is the most rewarding part of the project—much more rewarding than any money could be."

I peer up at her. "Is that why you did it—to change lives and help people?"

"That wasn't the original reason. It just worked out that way. More and more people started telling me about how it affected them—either by seeing other people be open and unashamed about their bodies or just by being in the show themselves."

"Why did you put yourself in the show?"

She shrugs. "It seemed like I couldn't really ask other people to do it if I wasn't ready to do it myself."

I catch myself casting a glance at her body. "It isn't like you have anything to be ashamed of."

She doesn't answer. At that moment, she rests her hand on my shoulder. Her touch sends a jet of fire through my insides, but I play it off like it's not that big a deal.

She leaves her hand there while we keep strolling down the pier—or she strolls. I roll. Walking with her like this makes me feel what it would be like if we were out here as a couple—if I really had a woman walking by my side.

She wouldn't just be any random woman. She would be my woman—the woman in my life. Is that what Mila is trying to imply?

Maybe she doesn't mean to imply that it could be her, but it sure does make me think what it could be like if someone did that.

She would walk next to me and rest her hand on my shoulder. It would be like what holding hands with a woman would be if I didn't have to use my hands to push my chair. It would be her way of staying connected with me while we walk.

The lights of New York glisten out of the darkness. They sparkle on the water and turn this into a romantic walk along the pier. I didn't ask her to come out with me to turn it into something romantic, but it's turning into that anyway.

I want it to. I want it to turn into something romantic, but I don't want to put that out there just in case she only came out to dinner with me as a casual get-together—which is what I said I wanted it to be.

I wouldn't want to step on her toes by making it more than that. I probably would have if I had taken her out before my accident—but then again, I wouldn't have taken her out before my accident. I wouldn't have been interested in her.

We come to the end of the pier and stop. She gazes up at all the lights shining in the darkness. Millions of lighted windows gleam out of every building.

"It's amazing to think that each of those windows represents a person," she murmurs. "Each one has a story to tell. It's amazing to think that people's lives are changing and becoming and falling apart behind each of those windows. Do you ever think about that? Do you ever think about all the stories that are happening in all those rooms all the time—around the clock—every hour of every day?"

I barely hear her. I stare up at her face from the side. She fascinates me. Her inner beauty completely eclipses how beautiful she is on the outside. I could never be good enough to make her interested in me.

My silence draws her attention. She turns around and looks straight down into my eyes. Her steady gaze made me uncomfortable when she interviewed me in my apartment.

She doesn't make me uncomfortable now. She can see all that I am with those clear, bright eyes of hers. I want her to see all that I am.

I don't hold out a hope in Hell that I'll ever be good enough for her, but I want her to see anyway. She floods me with relief that someone can see.

She knows more about how I think and feel than anyone I've ever met. I told her more in a few minutes during that interview than I've ever told anyone.

She stares back at me with the same intense, searching look. I get lost in her eyes—and then she bends down and kisses me before she stands up straight again.

"What was that for?" I ask.

"I knew you would never do it, so I did it first."

I don't know what to say. I never would have kissed her. Is it possible she feels the same way about me? She can't possibly think she isn't good enough for me.

We both turn around without discussing it first and walk all the way back to the restaurant. I call Andy to come pick us up.

She watches with the same fascinated interest when I use the board to get into the car. "What?" I ask.

"Nothing," she murmurs. "It's just so freakin' cool."

"Why is it cool? It's just the reality of how I have to get into and out of a car."

"I know. That's what's so cool about it." She shoots me a look. "It's way cooler than riding in a minivan."

I snort and the car pulls away from the curb. I want to take her hand on the ride home. I really want to kiss her, make out with her, and maybe make her climax right here on the limo seat.

I used to do stuff like that all the time. I can't do it with her.

I don't want to treat her like a piece of meat and I don't want her to treat me like one. I want her to love me—and I want to feel the same way about her.

My heart overflows when I think that about her. I want to feel that way about her. I just don't know how to. I don't even know if I'm mature enough to be capable of that.

Maybe I've squandered too much time—or maybe I'm too much of a player and a man-whore for her to ever consider me in that way.

I don't make a move on her. I absolutely refuse to turn tonight into that. She rested her hand on my shoulder and she kissed me. That's much farther than I would have been willing to take it. I can be satisfied with that.

The limo pulls up outside her building. I bend over to grab the board.

She lays her hand on my arm to stop me. "Don't. I'm sure I can get from here to the front door. You don't have to go to all that effort."

"I want to," I tell her. "I don't feel right about just sitting here."

"Well, I don't feel right about you going to all that trouble to get into your chair so we can say good night for thirty seconds before you have to get back into the car."

"It's no trouble," I tell her. "Really."

She darts forward and kisses me on the cheek this time. "I had a really nice time tonight. Thank you. I'll see you around."

She gets out of the car, rushes across the sidewalk to the door, unlocks it, and turns around to smile and wave at me before she ducks inside.

Now she's gone. I never got out of the limo.

My being revolts against that. I should have. I should have gotten out and walked her to the door—but it's too late now.

It's already close to midnight when Andy pulls the limo to the curb in front of the Nova Gallery. I go through the usual routine of getting out of the car and getting into my wheelchair.

A bunch of people stand around inside the gallery, but Mila isn't here. I just dropped her off at home after our date—or what I'm not calling a date.

I don't know anyone here and that's a good thing. I don't want to talk to anyone, especially not anyone I know.

I wheel over to the walls covered in the Infection display. I pass from one photograph to another searching everywhere for her, but she isn't here. Did she lie about putting herself in the show? Did she only say that to make me feel better?

I can't imagine her lying about anything, especially not that. She believes in this project. She would put herself in it first. She would have to if she hoped to convince other people to put themselves on public display, too.

I spend hours going from picture to picture. I don't spend too much time looking at the men, old people, and anyone with disfig-uring burns or facial deformities. I check every face. None of them is he r.

I finally come to the end of the display. I don't know why I'm suddenly so obsessed with her. It isn't because I want to see her naked.

These pictures….they affect me the same way now that they affected me before. I feel how deeply ashamed I am of my own body. I would never have the courage to let her photograph me. I don't want her or anyone else to see what I really look like.

I try to tell myself I'm not ashamed and that I'm okay with the way I am now—but I'm not okay with it, not really.

I try to dress it up by wearing suits all the time. I try to look as good as I possibly can on the outside. That's the only way I can stand to show myself in public.

She's the one who shines a light on this shame. She's the one who makes me realize that it's okay. If I have a prayer of getting over this, it will be thanks to her.

I leave the gallery. Seeing her picture wouldn't tell me anything I want to know—not really. She's so open and honest about everything and yet I still can't find out the one thing about her that I really want to know. I don't even know what that is.

I suppose the only question in my mind is if she could actually feel anything for me. I want to believe she could, but I might be deluding myself about that. She might have said that to make me feel better, too—or I might just be too degenerate for someone like her.

It doesn't matter. I made up my mind after the accident that I might spend the rest of my life alone—and I'm okay with that. I can live with it. I have enough going on in the rest of my life. I don't need a relationship.

It sure would be nice, though. She sure is nice.

I head back outside to the limo. I'm already getting tired. It's way too late for me to be dwelling on this. Maybe I'm only obsessing over it because it's late and I'm tired. Maybe I won't care about any of this once I go home and get some sleep.

I roll out of the gallery and stop on the sidewalk. Andy doesn't see me at first. He sits behind the wheel playing some video game on his phone.

I rap my knuckles on the window and he jumps out of his skin. He scrambles to get out of the car to help me.

Right then, another guy barges up to me on the sidewalk. God only knows what he's doing out here at this time of night.

"Hey!" he snaps at me. "I saw you with Mila Knapp before."

I look up at him. He's a beefy guy with a five o'clock shadow. He has a sloppy, disheveled look like he has to remind himself to take a shower once a week.

He doesn't look like he's actually drunk at this moment, but he looks like someone who commits far too much of his time to making it his long-term hobby.

"Yeah?" I ask. "So?"

"So I'm her boyfriend and you're nothing." He bends over and points in my face. "You keep away from her if you know what's good for you."

I snort at him and pull my chair away. "Don't worry, pal. I never laid a finger on her."

The guy hauls off and punches me square in the jaw. I'm not even facing him when it happens. He hits me so hard and so fast that he completely knocks my chair over and sends me sprawling on the ground.

He pounces on me swinging for the fences. Andy dives in to help me, but that first hit ignites all the fury I've been holding down all these months. I never let myself feel before just how enraged I am that this happened to me.

That one punch lets the beast off its chain and I go completely berserk. I grab the guy a lot harder than I plan to.

I barely feel it when I flip him over, slam him down on the pavement, and drive my elbow into his face again and again. I don't even take the time to sit up all the way. I'm too furious even for that.

I hit him five or six times before Andy gets there. He grabs for my arms trying to pull me away from the guy. I shake Andy off and hit the guy again before Andy finally pins my arms down.

"Hey! Hold up!!" Andy yells at me. "Hey, Mr. Nowaczyk! Hey—Giovanni! Hold up! Stop now! He's down! He's down!"

This is the first time he's ever called me by my first name. He always calls me, 'Sir,' or he uses my last name if he calls me anything at all. His voice snaps me out of my frenzy.

Blood pours from the guy's nose and mouth. He's out cold on the pavement.

Andy doesn't wait around for me to pull my head out of the fog. He straightens up, sets my wheelchair on its wheels, locks the brakes, and heaves me into the seat. My jaw hurts and I taste blood in my mouth.

He gets on his phone and calls the Police. We have to sit here and wait for them to come. Then they call an ambulance.

We go through another few hours of nonsense waiting for the gallery owner to show up. The place has a security camera mounted directly over the door. The Police go inside and find footage of the whole incident.

A plain-clothes cop comes over to me after the officers watch the footage. "We'll place the assailant under arrest and apply for a restraining order to keep him away from you."

I look away. "Fine."

"Can you tell me why he attacked you?"

"I took a girl out to dinner earlier tonight. He says he's her boyfriend, but she never told me anything about it. I guess it was my mistake."

"Not really. She should have said something."

"It doesn't matter. It's over. Can I go now?"

"Sure," the cop tells me. "Have a good one."

I snort to myself and get busy getting back into my car. Coming here tonight was a colossal mistake. Everything about my association with Mila was a mistake if she could lie to me about something like this.

Chapter 10: Mila

I'm just coming out of the photography supply store when a man walks up to me on the street. He's a few inches taller than I am with tussled brown hair and a few days' growth of stubble.

He wears a plaid flannel shirt, jeans, and he walks around with his boots untied. "Hey!" he snaps at me.

I turn around and raise my eyebrows when I see his face covered in bruises. He has two black eyes, a broken nose, and his lips swell up with cracks and blood blisters. "What the hell happened to you, Connor?"

"What the hell do you think happened to me?" he fires back. "You set me up!"

I furrow my brow. "I what?"

"You went out with that asshole boyfriend of yours Giovanni Nowaczyk and he beat me up!"

I snort at him and turn away to walk off down the street. "Giovanni isn't my boyfriend and neither are you, Connor. When are you going to learn to leave it alone?"

"Hey! I'm talking to you!" He grabs my arm and turns me around. "What the hell is the matter with you? I told you not to keep messing with me like this."

"I'm not messing with you, Connor. I've told you before and I'll keep telling you until you get it through your thick head. We aren't together. We never have been. You have no reason to go around confronting people I may or may not be going out with."

"You kissed him!"

"So what if I did? It's none of your business if I kissed him or someone else." I realize what I'm saying. "Wait a minute. You confronted Giovanni....and he beat you up? Are you saying he jumped out of his wheelchair and hit you? Something tells me that didn't happen."

"Take a look at my goddamn face, you bitch! Do you think I just fell over and bumped my head on the sidewalk?"

"How did it happen?" I hold up my hand. "Don't tell me. You hit him first, didn't you?"

"That's no reason he should do *this* to me!" He waves at his face. "He could have killed me! Even the cops said so."

"You.....hit a guy.....in a wheelchair?" I roll my eyes to heaven. "This is a new low for you, Connor."

"Hey! Don't you walk away from me!"

"I have to go to work. See you later."

I walk away still shaking my head. I can't believe it. Connor actually attacked a man in a wheelchair.

Good for Giovanni for defending himself. I don't blame him for overreacting. It looks like he taught Connor a lesson.

I head down the street, collect a bunch of photography gear from my apartment, and return to Central Park. I have a photoshoot with a family today. I meet them at Glade Arch and we head out to an open field where we start the shoot.

I eventually move them to one of the walkways and then on top of the arch itself. I'm in the middle of taking pictures when I notice what looks like a filming crew working in another part of the park.

They're working near the fountain—and then I see a man in a wheelchair buzzing around the whole set. He points to things and gives orders to everyone.

I can't see or hear what they're doing over there, but he has his work and I have mine. I concentrate on finishing working with the family and I show them some of the stills on the digital display of my camera.

The family is thrilled with the results. I plan to email them the proofs for them to choose their final choices. They leave and I start packing up my gear.

I'm just putting my tripods and lighting rigs away when Giovanni comes up to me on top of the arch. I smile at him. "Hey!" I exclaim.

He doesn't smile back. "Why didn't you tell me you have a boyfriend?" he demands. "Why did you kiss me and act all close to me the other night if you were already involved with someone? How could you lead me on like that?"

I groan and cover my eyes. "Connor is not my boyfriend, Giovanni. I don't know what he told you...."

"That's what he said. He said he's your boyfriend and he threatened me to keep away from you."

"Well, he isn't my boyfriend. He's a lowlife scumbag—just in case we all didn't know that." I shoot a sidelong glance at the bruise on his jaw. "I'm sorry you got caught in the middle of it."

"How can I believe you when he's going around getting in my face saying he is?" he asks.

I straighten up and face him. I have to stop myself from taking out my annoyance on him. He isn't involved in this—except that he is.

"You'll be happy to know that Connor called *you* my boyfriend," I tell him. "What does that tell you? He's delusional."

"I don't believe you," he counters. "I can't believe anything you tell me now. Was anything you told me the truth?"

"I can prove it to you."

"How? How would you do that?"

I shrug and go back to organizing my stuff. "That depends on whether you're even interested enough to listen to me. If you are, I can show you. If you really can't trust me, then I don't even know why you're here asking me about it. He isn't my boyfriend. I would have told you if he was and I never would have agreed to go out with you. It's up to you. I'm not going to fall on bended knee and beg you to believe me."

"Prove it, then. Give me something that will convince me you're sincere—about any of this."

I glance at him and stuff the rest of my gear into my equipment bags. "Fine. I'll do it, but I have to take this stuff home first."

"Bring it here. I'll drive you."

I heft all my gear into my arms. I only have to carry it to the edge of the park before Andy comes to pick us up in the limo. He puts everything in the trunk.

I try not to notice that I'm driving around in Giovanni's limo again. We had such a nice date. I know now that it really was a date even if he played it off and pretended that it wasn't.

I go inside my apartment to put my gear away. When I come out, Giovanni is sitting in his wheelchair on the sidewalk. Andy and the limo are nowhere in sight.

Giovanni looks up at me. His eyes speak volumes. He's confused, hurt, and angry—exactly the way he would be if he had taken me out and started to get ideas about us—only to find out I was already seeing someone on the side.

"Where are we going?" he asks.

I wave to the right and we set off walking through town. I can't even make a joke about him walking with his arms. Nothing about him is funny. He's a regular man with a heart and soul that can hurt like anyone else.

"I'm really sorry about what happened with Connor," I murmur on the way. "I'm sorry you got caught in the middle of this."

"I'm not in the middle of anything. You're either with him or you aren't. If you are, then I'm out. If you aren't, then there's no middle to get caught in."

"I meant I'm sorry he hit you. I'm sorry you even had to find out that he exists."

He snorts under his breath. "He's the one who's sorry he hit me."

I don't answer that. I sure hope Connor is smart enough to realize how colossally he messed up. Maybe he thought Giovanni couldn't fight back because he's paralyzed. Now Connor realizes he can't just go around getting violent with anyone he chooses.

I stop in front of the Nova Gallery and take the keys out of my pocket.

"What are we doing here?" Giovanni asks.

"You said you wanted proof." I unlock the door and hold it open for him. "Come on in."

He wheels in and I lock the door behind us so no one thinks the gallery is open. I lead him to the Infection display, stop next to one of the walls, and take down one of the pictures.

I hold it out to him and he takes it. I don't even have to look at it to know what he's seeing.

The picture is of me lying naked on my back on my bed and staring up into the camera directly above my face as if someone is looking down at me from the ceiling.

My hair splays out from my head in a big, flowing, watery mermaid style. I stare up at the camera with my arms raised above my head.

I'm missing half of one breast and half of the muscle on my outer left thigh. The rest of me looks normal. He doesn't react. He just stares down at the picture. He's a million miles away.

"I had a lumpectomy four years ago," I tell him. "I had to have a bunch of lymph nodes and other tissue removed at the same time. I had a case of necrotizing fasciitis when I was a kid. The doctors had to remove part of my leg to save my life. I started photographing myself as a way to try to reclaim some sense of myself as an attractive, sexual being instead of some kind of Quasimodo elephant woman which is what I thought I was. I thought I was hideous and disgusting. I took dozens of pictures of myself and threw them all away before I found one that I thought actually made me look beautiful. The whole process helped me get over all of that and accept myself. That's how I started doing the Infection Project. I started doing the pictures privately with friends and people I just randomly met in public. I offered to do it for them for free just as a way to help them deal with the shame they had toward their bodies. It grew into all of this. I went on three dates with Connor and kissed him once. He dumped me when I had the surgery on my breast. He only started coming around making a nuisance of himself after I started to get some notoriety for the Infection show and started to make some money from my photography. He isn't my boyfriend and he never was. We never got serious before he ended it."

Giovanni looks up and holds out the picture to give it back. "You are beautiful," he tells me.

"So are you. Whatever it is you're hiding under that fancy suit is just as beautiful as I am."

He looks away and winds up glancing at all the pictures. I can't read his reaction to what I said. I hang the picture back in its place. It's at the height of my shoulders, so maybe he just didn't see it before.

I'm just turning around when he rolls toward me, stops, and slips his hand into mine. "I'm sorry I doubted you. I had a feeling from the beginning that you were sincere. I shouldn't have confronted you—not like that. I could have found out about him without calling you a liar and implying that you were messing with me."

"I'm just really sorry this happened. I've told him a million times to back off. He never listens."

He squeezes my hand and his features start to soften. He stops himself from smiling. "I'm just now realizing that the logistics of me sitting in a wheelchair are going to demand that I come up with a whole new strategy when I meet a woman I like."

"A new strategy for doing what? You seem to be doing just fine from where I'm standing."

"That's the problem. You're standing and I'm sitting. I can't just move in and kiss you the way I would if we were both standing."

I get a stomach full of butterflies when I see the look in his eyes. "Would you kiss me right now if you were standing up?"

"Absolutely." He tugs my hand. "Sit down on my lap."

Adrenaline pumps through my veils, but I don't hold back. I want to get close to him. This has been coming since we first met. I didn't let myself see it then—except that he's so drop-dead attractive.

I swivel sideways and sit down on his lap. He sets the brakes so his chair doesn't move.

I ease my weight down on him and put my arm behind his neck. He finally lets himself smile up at me and he slips his arms around my waist. He doesn't try to touch me in any other way. "This feels good," he remarks.

"Remember when you said you had nerve damage in your legs?" I ask.

"How could I forget?"

"Do you have feeling in your legs?"

"Of course."

"I mean how much feeling do you have in your legs?"

"All of it," he replies. "I have full sensation in my whole body. I just can't move them. That's all."

"So.....does it hurt when I sit on your legs like this?"

He smiles at me and color washes over his cheeks. "I just said it feels good."

"You know what I mean. There's good and then there's good."

He laughs and bites it back. "I wouldn't tell you if it did hurt."

"I wouldn't want to sit on your lap if it hurt you."

"I would want you to sit on my lap even if it did hurt me. I want you here."

I try to look away, but I can't break eye contact. My heart flips and my voice breaks when I try to speak. "What's going to happen to us?"

He gets serious real quick and his eyes go hard. He stares back at me for a minute and then slips his fingers into my hair to kiss me.

We kiss much deeper, hotter, and longer this time. My eyes drift closed in the bottomless, sultry velvet of his lips and tongue.

Sitting on his lap like this turns me on. I want him. My body buzzes for him, but I can't make the first move.

Sitting on his lap makes me feel small, fragile, and vulnerable. I'm in his arms and in his hands. He responds the same way. He seems to get bigger and swell with powerful strength and energy.

His arm tightens behind my back and his breath catches. I pant into his mouth as the tension rises. He isn't even doing anything—and then his hand slides up my back to my neck.

That ever-so-soft grip melts me in his hands. I need him. I need him to hold me and kiss me like this. I need his hands rubbing down my arms and up my thigh to my hip.

He pulls me tighter against him and I feel him start to get hard. He grasps my thigh—the one closest to his body. He grips it hard halfway up from my knee and sends a lightning bolt of molten desire straight to my core.

He lets go just as fast, pulls off my mouth breathing hard, and straightens up to look into my eyes. His features smolder with barely contained primal, ravenous hunger. He rasped through his teeth. "I want you.....but I don't want to offend you."

"You won't," I tell him. I find myself touching his jacket. "I want you, too."

He gulps and looks away. "I can't treat you like that. You mean too much to me."

"No one is going to make you do something you don't want to do. You don't have to do anything you don't want to do."

"I do want to....but kissing you only makes me want you more."

Now I'm the one who leans and kisses him. I want to do a lot more than that, but I understand why he holds back. He doesn't want to repeat the mistakes of his past. He wants to change.

He finally pulls away, but he won't raise his eyes to look at me. I stroke his face and hair. He's immaculate exactly the way he is.

"Are you okay?" I murmur. "I can get off if my weight is bothering you."

His eyes dart up. He acts like he didn't hear me. "I want you to go out with me again—on a real date this time. I don't want to pretend it's something else."

I smile at him. I love how earnest he is about all of this. It shows he's serious and wants it to mean something. "I'd like that. I would love to go out with you."

He glances down at me and taps me on the arm. "Stand up and I'll walk you home."

Chapter 11: Giovanni

I call Mila on the phone. "I'm outside."

"I'm on my way," she replies.

I turn my wheelchair around to survey the neighborhood while I wait. I keep looking around for that dipshit Connor. I might have to break his face again if he tries anything else.

I spin the other way when I hear her open the door. She comes out all glowing in a beautiful black dress. It's knee-length so it hides her leg.

I didn't feel anything out of the ordinary when I touched her the other night, but the missing part of her left thigh was toward me. I wouldn't have felt it.

She must wear some kind of padded bra because her top half looks normal. No one would ever guess she had anything wrong with her. I can't even call it something wrong with her because she's magnificent the way she is.

I've spent the last week fantasizing about what she looked like in that picture. She looks like some kind of goddess. She is a goddess.

She's angelic. Her scars only make her more beautiful. I understand what she means about that now.

I don't want to think about someone seeing me like that—except that I know she would. She could photograph me to look like that. She could show that my disability, my scars, and my bony legs are just as attractive to her as she is to me.

I'm not ready to start thinking about that yet. I'm still too over the moon thinking about her.

I smile up at her and she smiles down at me. Her cheeks color. "Hi," she breathes.

"Hi," I murmur. "You look outstanding."

She blushes. "So do you."

I take her hand. I don't even want to get into the car. I just want to sit here and stare at her as much as possible.

She laughs at my reaction. "Are we going?"

"Do we have to?"

She laughs. "Is this the whole date, then?"

I can't help but laugh along with her. I steer her over to the car and she gets in. I slide in next to her and Andy puts my chair away before he shuts the door.

Mila and I hold hands on the way down the street. I can't stop staring into her eyes.

"How are you doing?" she asks.

"I'm doing good. How are you?"

She blushes again. "I'm good. What have you been up to?"

I shrug and look away. "I guess we have to have a normal conversation. I've been trying to straighten out my company."

She frowns. "What's wrong with it? It's one of the most highly respected media companies in the world."

"I don't know what's wrong with it—except that everything is wrong with it. I guess you could say the company is a reflection of myself and I'm only just realizing how shallow and meaningless it all is compared to your work. Everything about me and my life was shallow and meaningless. I shouldn't even be surprised that the company turned out to be that way, too."

"But your company isn't even in the same category as my work. My work is artistic photography...."

"That's exactly my point. It isn't artistic....but it should be."

She makes a face at me. "I think you'll find that almost everyone else in the world thinks your work *is* artistic. You're one of the most artistic people I've ever met."

"It isn't the same. I want it to mean something. I've been trying to inspire the photographers and designers to make it more artistic, but they just don't get what I mean—probably because I don't know what I mean. I don't understand how to make it have depth when I've never had depth before."

"You do have depth." She squeezes my hand. "You have a lot of depth."

"But what is that depth? Maybe I don't have depth and this is all just me realizing that I don't."

"I don't see it that way at all."

"How do you see it?" I ask. "What makes you think I have depth?"

"You said my work moved you."

"It did."

"That's what I mean. You may not have explored these deeper layers of yourself, but I'm certain they're there. That's what this is. You've dropped into a deeper level of yourself—a level you don't understand—but it is there. You're there now. You aren't as superficial and shallow as you were. The person you were before never would have said no to me the other night."

I look away. "You're right. I wouldn't have."

"The person you were before probably couldn't have said no to me the other night even if you knew it was wrong. You wouldn't have been able to stop yourself."

I wince. "I don't want to talk about that."

She laces her fingers into mine. "We don't have to."

"I don't mean that," I blurt out. "It's just....embarrassing."

"But you aren't like that anymore. You did say no. You've been very honest that you wanted to treat me with the respect you should have shown those girls before."

I can't look at her. "I shouldn't have been anywhere near them. I never should have had anything to do with them."

"I don't think you should compare yourself to the person you were before. You obviously aren't that person anymore. Isn't that kind of what you told me during your interview? You've changed. The accident changed you. You aren't that person anymore. You don't have access to those girls anymore—and that's for the best. You grew up a lot and became the person you were supposed to become." She squeezes my hand tighter. "I wouldn't be sitting here right now if the accident hadn't happened. You wouldn't be anyone I would be interested in."

"That's the most embarrassing part," I mumble.

She leans over and kisses me on the forehead. "You're wonderful the way you are now—and now you're going on a new artistic journey. It's a good thing. You're discovering new dimensions of yourself just like I am. I never would have started Infection if all those things had never happened to me."

I have to look up at her. She always brings it full circle and makes it mean something. She always makes it make sense. That's her superpower.

"Thank you," I murmur. "For all of this."

"You're giving me something just as valuable. Don't you understand that? What you're giving me is just as important as what I'm giving you."

"What am I giving you?" I ask. "You're the one who's giving me my life back."

"You're giving me acceptance. You're accepting me and appreciating me and admiring me even though I have these flaws that society says make me unlovable. Society says these imperfections make me hideous and deformed and disgusting and undatable."

I snort. "That's exactly what they *don't* make you."

"But that's what you're giving me. It's one thing for me to accept myself and to be okay with putting my picture on a wall full of hundreds of other pictures. It's something else for a man to actually see me naked and still find me attractive and want to be with me. That's taking a huge risk. It would be easy for me to just keep to myself and never date again for the rest of my life. I could call that accepting myself, but I wouldn't be. It would just be a deeper level of shame."

"You are attractive. You're gorgeous."

"That's what you're giving me—the same way I'm giving it to you. You're giving me back the life I thought I lost when I had the surgery. Connor said he couldn't stand to look at me....."

"What a jackass!" I exclaim. "He did not actually say that!"

She nods and smiles at me. "Yep—but your girls are saying the same thing when they don't look at you. They're basically saying the same thing without actually saying it—and they don't even know what you look like underneath, do they? They haven't seen you since the accident. Have they?"

I look away again. "No. No one has seen me."

She slips her hand onto my leg. "Would you like me too? I'll show you mine if you show me yours."

I spin around fast and see her gazing at me with all the same molten desire I saw in her eyes that night at the gallery. I want her so bad. I want to attack her and ravage her and conquer her, but I don't want to insult her or use her or show her any disrespect.

I respect her more than I ever thought I could respect anyone. I want to honor her. I want to put her on a pedestal and make the whole world worship her the way I do.

Andy pulls the limo up in front of the restaurant right then. The process of getting out of the car lets me off the hook from answering her question.

I want to see her naked. I want to enjoy all the delights of her naked body and for her to enjoy mine, but I don't want to ruin anything by going too far too fast. I'm prepared to wait as long as it takes.

She rests her hand on my shoulder on our way inside. I get that feeling again that we're already a couple. She's my girlfriend or fiancé or wife and this is her way of staying linked with me while we walk into wherever we're walking into.

This is her way of showing the world that she's mine and I'm hers. This is her way of announcing to the world that we're a couple and nothing will tear us apart.

I love that feeling. I can't get enough of it. I want her to walk around everywhere like that. I want to feel her hand on my shoulder and know that she's mine and I'm hers.

Her hand tells me she's proud of me. It tells me she's proud of what I am and she's proud to be with me. Nothing could be wrong with that.

I must be doing something right if she treats me like this. I can't do anything to jeopardize that, even if it means waiting until doomsday before I can have her.

I don't want her for one night. I want her forever. I want the whole world to know she's the only one. I consider it a privilege to go without while I wait for her.

We enter a much quieter, darker, more private restaurant. I've had to eliminate all the non-accessible restaurants from my repertoire. This disability has made me have to get creative and patronize restaurants I never would have patronized before.

This is a sultry Russian restaurant that occupies the top floor of a business complex downtown. Not many people know about this establishment. I get the feeling it caters to a lot of bratva clientele.

I suspect the restaurant management only caters to me because I tip extra well. They go out of their way to accommodate me, especially now.

I've made special arrangements to bring Mila here, so the manager and waitstaff go over the top to take good care of us.

Two other couples sit at tables on the opposite side of the restaurant. They don't look up when Mila and I walk in all dressed up.

The manager leads us to a table with two place settings and only one chair. Mila beams at me across the table and takes my hand again. The candlelight reflects on her cheeks when she smiles.

"This is so much nicer than the other restaurant—not that the other restaurant wasn't nice. It just wasn't as intimate."

"How long has it been since you've gone on a date like this?"

She grimaces. "I've never been on a date like this. You want the truth? There it is. No one has ever taken me out the way you have."

"I haven't been on a date like this before, either," I tell her. "We can figure it out together."

She blushes. "That makes me feel better."

"I'm glad I can give you some nice experiences you've never had before."

"Me, too. I hope this lives up to the hype after all the excitement you were having before."

I scoff at that. "What I had before doesn't even come close to this. They aren't even in the same solar system."

She laughs. "In a good way or a bad way?"

"This is way better. Knowing you and getting to know you—thinking I might actually stand a chance with you—it's like nothing I've ever felt—and don't tell me yet if I don't stand a chance with you. Let me live in my little fantasy world a little longer."

She splits in a grin and squeezes my hand. "You stand a chance with me. Don't worry—and I should be saying the same thing. Don't you know what all the trade periodicals are saying about what a great catch you are?"

Now it's my turn to make a face. "They only say that because they don't know me—or maybe they do. They think some hot megastar is going to come along, knock my socks off, and make me clean up my act. No one thinks it might happen the other way around."

"I have to be honest. I never pictured myself getting together with a billionaire."

"It's not all it's cracked up to be."

She frowns. "Do the other club members have a hard time staying in relationships? Does their money interfere?"

"Not at all. They're dedicated family men—and women. I have some good role models. It's just a shame that I haven't had the brains to follow their example in the past."

"What are they like?" she asks. "What kind of people are they?"

"They're the best kind of people. Hey, I just had an idea. You should come to our next gala—as my date. Then you could meet them all. They're good people. They would love to meet you."

"What makes you say that? Are they into photography?"

I laugh. "No, not because of that—although I have heard some of them mention your show. They're all extremely impressed by you. They would be thrilled if they knew I was dating you."

She blushes again. "Is that what you're doing?"

"I'm taking you on dates, aren't I? Isn't that what dating is?"

"There's going on dates and then there's dating."

I shrug. "So what do you say to coming to the gala with me."

She smiles. "I would love to. I would love to go anywhere with you."

"Now you're going to give me a complex."

"Since we're dating, maybe you could come with me to an occasion I'm attending. You could be my date."

"I would love to. What's the occasion?"

"I'm receiving an award."

My head shoots up. "You are?"

She dips her eyelashes and looks away. "It's the Annie Leibowitz Award for Excellence in Photography."

My jaw drops. "Wow."

She won't stop blushing to the roots of her hair. "I know. I don't know how I feel about anyone comparing me to Annie Leibowitz."

"You are!" I breathe. "I've thought that before."

"Naw," she chides.

"Yes! You are! You're going to accept it, aren't you? You have to!"

"Oh, yeah. I'm already on the list and I've already RSVPed to say I'm going. Now I just have to get up in front of the world and have everyone stare at me."

"You deserve it. Your work is every bit as good as hers and it means something so much more."

She looks away and the waiter intervenes just then by coming over to our table to take our order.

I can't stop staring at her through the candlelight. I'm proud of her. I'm proud to be taking her out. I'm proud to have her by my side. I would be over-the-top proud to call her mine and to let the world see us together.

I can't wait for all of that. I can't wait to take her to one of the club galas as my date.

I've always taken hired girls or just any girl who wanted to go for the night. I've never taken an actual date—as in someone that I've been going out with. I've never even gone out with anyone—not like this.

The world is going to find out pretty soon that I'm seeing someone. The world is going to go bananas when they see me attending her awards ceremony and applauding her achievements along with the rest of the crowd.

No one will wonder how she landed me and made me get serious all of a sudden. They'll think she did it by being such an outstanding person. No one will ever find out that it happened the other way around.

Chapter 12: Mila

Giovanni and I get into the back of his limo. Waiting for him to slide across from one seat to another, put his board away, and then waiting for Andy to put Giovanni's wheelchair away—it all seems so normal now. I hardly remember doing it any other way.

Giovanni smiles at me while he adjusts his position on the seat next to me. His chest, back, and shoulders swell with muscle when he pushes himself up on his arms.

His shirt strains across his chest and shows how strong he is. He must be if he beat up Connor the way he did.

Giovanni slips his hand into mine. "Tonight was a dream come true for me," he murmurs. "I can't wait for the next time. I can't wait to take you out in public and show you off."

I blush. "I don't know what people are going to think when they find out I'm dating a billionaire."

"Am I so different because of that?"

I can't stop smiling at him. "Not because of that."

His eyes go hard and he leans in and kisses me. I get lost in the warmth of his lips. He lets go of my hand, touches my cheek, and then those powerful arms encircle me, lift me off the seat, and sit me across his lap the way he did the other night.

He kisses me faster and harder this time. His breath comes faster and more strained. He doesn't try as hard to hold himself under control or to hide how passionate he feels. He really must have been going crazy all these months.

He breaks off my mouth and dives into my neck kissing me in hot, scorching mouthfuls. I gasp and whimper as the energy between us escalates. He doesn't stop. His ravenous fury excites me. I want more of it.

He strokes me all over my dress and comes dangerously close to my breasts, but he stops short of actually touching me. He runs his hands up my bare shins to my knees and squeezes—just enough to make me sob and tremble in his arms.

I want him to touch me. I want him inside me. I want him to take me and fill me with more pleasure than I can't stand it—but I don't want to push him to do something he isn't comfortable with.

He straightens his head and his eyes drift open so full of overpowering volcanic madness. He looks dangerous like this—and intoxicating. I melt at that look. My thighs want to sag open to let him in.

"Mmmm," he murmurs. "You're delicious. I can never get enough of you."

"Are you ever going to let yourself take me? How long are you going to keep punishing yourself?"

His eyes narrow just a little bit. He scrapes his teeth across his lower lip and looks down at my body. "As long as I can possibly restrain myself."

"What if I want you to before that? What if I asked you to?"

His eyes lock on me. "Is that really what you want?"

"Of course. I want you to show me that you find me attractive and appealing."

"I find you attractive and appealing. I find you irresistible."

"Don't you want to know if I find you attractive and appealing?"

He looks down at my mouth and then at his own hand traveling up and down my sides. "Yes," he murmurs. "I would give anything to believe that you find me as attractive and appealing as I find you."

"How would I be able to convince you of that if I didn't show you in person?"

He looks up one more time. "Are you sure you want that?"

Now I'm the one who looks away. "I would show you right now if I thought you wanted me to—but I know you don't want me to. It would only make you uncomfortable."

"What would you do to show me in a way that I would be comfortable with?"

"I would take you home and undress you and worship your body. I would cover you in my body and fill you with so much pleasure that you had no choice but to believe it."

"That's what I want to do to you," he breathes. He cups my cheeks and looks deep into my eyes. "I want to give you everything. I want to make you believe how beautiful and angelic you are."

I sink into kissing him for the ages. His hands drive me wild coming so close to touching me and then backing off. He never lets himself touch me even though I want him to.

He pulls back and we float in each other's eyes.

"Would you let me touch you?" I ask.

His eyebrows fly up. "Here?"

"Anywhere. Do you plan to do everything while I lie there and let you do it? Would you ever let me touch you?"

He looks away again. He won't hold eye contact except at certain times. "Would you ever be with me in a way that you would accept it if I didn't let you touch me?"

"No, I wouldn't. If we're doing this, then I would have to touch you. I wouldn't want to do anything with you if you weren't comfortable with that."

He nods. "That's what I expected."

I wilt in relief. "Good. I was worried."

He laughs. "You were worried I wouldn't let you touch me?"

I nod. "I thought you would hold me at a distance even then."

"When have I ever held you at a distance? I've been trying to get close to you since the beginning. I just didn't know how to do it because I've never done anything like this before."

"Maybe that's what I saw as you holding me at a distance."

He moves in on me. "I don't want to hold you at a distance...and I want you to touch me."

I jolt back. "You do?"

"I'm not gonna lie. It scares the shit out of me, but yes. I want you to. Something tells me I need you to. It will heal me. You will heal me. I need that."

I don't know what to say. I don't see myself as healing anyone—but I guess I am.

He startles me back to reality by kissing me again, and this time, I slip my hand inside his jacket. His body shudders when I touch him through his shirt. His muscles tense and he trembles.

I love that feeling that I can affect him so much. I want to touch his bare skin, but now isn't the time and place.

We seem to have developed this unspoken rule that we won't take each other's clothes off or do anything overtly sexual while we're in the car—much as we both might want to.

He finally tears away and puts me back on the seat next to him. His eyes burn with so much suggestive fire.

He turns aside and pushes a button on his door to lower the window that separates us from the driver's compartment. "Mila is coming home with me tonight, Andy," Giovanni calls. "You can take us straight back to my place."

"You got it, Sir!" Andy calls without turning around.

Giovanni rolls up the window and turns back to me. "Now you get to see my vampire crypt in all its nighttime glory."

I laugh. "Is it really that different from what it looks like in daylight?"

"It's an inside joke between me and the guys at the club. They tease me because I don't go out as much as I used to."

"You've gone out in daylight plenty of times that I've seen. You were at the park in daylight the other day."

"True."

"So what's in the rest of your labyrinth?" I ask. "What else is on that floor of the building? Is that where your coven stores all their coffins?"

He laughs. "One of the rooms is a sauna. One is my home gym. There's a separate office I sometimes use. That floor has all kinds of nooks and crannies for different things. One of the doors leads to a whole separate self-contained guest apartment in case I want to get rid of a guest or they just can't stand to stay in the same apartment with me any longer."

"Who would that be? Do you have a mother-in-law from Hell or something?"

He laughs again. "I don't have any mother-in-law at all, but I do have a mother who occasionally comes to visit me."

My head shoots up. "You do? Where is she?"

"She lives with my dad in Queens. My older brother and his wife and kids live out there, too. They're as middle-class as you could possibly want."

"That is so sweet! Do you visit them a lot?"

"No, they always come to visit me. They seem to think I'm too busy to go visit them or maybe they think I'm too good for my humble beginnings. My parents would never let me stay over at their house. They would be humiliated."

"Aw. That's sad."

"I don't bring it up. I don't want to embarrass them, so they always come to visit me."

"I guess that makes sense. How do they feel about your accident?"

He winces. "They also have a tendency to be a lot more sensitive about it than I am. It's really hard to talk to my mom when she's constantly suggesting that she come over and help me with anything—whatever that might be. She would be over here day and night cooking and cleaning for me if I let her. She seems to think I'm crumbling into decay without constant care and attention."

"Wow. That has to be hard."

Andy drives into the parking garage under Giovanni's apartment building just then, parks, and we get out of the car.

Andy places Giovanni's wheelchair for him and leaves immediately. Andy walks across the parking garage and gets into the elevator without waiting for Giovanni to finish.

"Where is he going?" I ask. "What if something happens and you need help with something?"

"I have a phone. I can call him back. Oh, I forgot to tell you. One of those doors up there leads to another apartment where he lives."

"He lives here—on the same floor with you?"

"He's on call around the clock in case I want to go anywhere. That's the arrangement we have. He has his own apartment, but he has to be available. He can do whatever he wants when I don't need him as long as he's there when I do need him. He gets a copy of my schedule so he knows when I plan to come and go every day—or if I don't plan to come and go every day. He gets the rest of the time off."

"That's....interesting."

"It works for both of us." He slides the board back onto the limo seat and slams the passenger door. I guess that's all we need to do.

Chapter 13: Mila

Giovanni rolls his wheelchair over to the elevator. I stand next to him while we wait. The elevator is still on the way up to deliver Andy to the forty-ninth floor.

Giovanni reads my mind. "We have this unspoken agreement between us that we go home separately. We don't ride up the elevator together. It helps us both maintain the illusion that we don't live together and we aren't going home as a couple."

I laugh. "I can definitely see how that would be important—especially if you're bringing someone home with you. It would be super awkward if he rode up in the elevator with us."

He slips his hand into mine. "I'm really happy about tonight. I can't imagine anything better than this."

"We can take it slowly. We don't have to rush into anything if you get nervous and want to change your mind."

He cocks his head. "Are *you* getting nervous?"

"I'm petrified. Are you kidding me?"

He bursts into a grin. "Me, too."

"You don't act like it. You act like you're calm, cool, and collected."

"I have to act that way to stop you from seeing how scared I am. I'm trying to be confident, controlled, and reassuring."

I look away. "I'm glad someone is."

The elevator stops on the forty-ninth floor and starts coming down again.

"So how will we do it?" he asks. "Will we play strip poker?"

I make a face and wind up laughing, but my nerves are seriously starting to get the better of me. "Something tells me that wouldn't be such a great idea."

He doesn't break the silence until the elevator comes. We both get in. I can't look at him, not even when he takes my hand again. He's being a lot more confident and reassuring than I am. Will I actually be able to go through with this without completely losing my nerve?

The elevator takes ages to climb all the way up to his floor. The silence becomes oppressive.

He startles me by asking. "What about you? Is your family in New York?"

"They live in Jersey. I see them pretty often. My parents and my brother-in-law are all in the Infection show, so that brings us closer together."

His head shoots up. "They are?"

I nod. "My mom had breast cancer ten years ago—so it runs in the family. My dad is a combat veteran and has a ton of surgery scars—so they were some of the very first people I photographed."

"What about your brother-in-law?"

"He and my sister got married straight out of high school. They were childhood sweethearts and always knew they would marry each other one day. They weren't planning to do it so soon. They both planned to go to college after high school, but she got pregnant the summer they graduated, so they decided to tie the knot and go to college together anyway. They made it one year before they got hit by a drunk driver and she got killed along with the baby. He survived, of course, and now he's married to someone else with three kids—but he's still a part of our family. His family comes over for Christmas, Easter, Thanksgiving, birthdays—everything—as if he was my real brother."

"Does he have scars? Did he get hurt in the accident?"

"The windshield shattered in his face and he got a bunch of tiny little scars all over his face. Most people don't even know they're there. You would never know if you met him, but a lot of people in the show don't have any kind of scars or deformity or anything like that. They're just normal people who still have a lot of insecurity about their bodies."

He faces front. "I saw that."

The elevator doors open and we step out into the hall. I don't see which of the other doors is Andy's apartment. I don't ask. I don't want to know. He deserves his privacy.

Giovanni leads me to his penthouse where he unlocks the door with an electronic card. He pushes the door open, rolls through it, and holds the door open for me to enter.

Automatic motion sensors switch on the lights as soon as we walk in. The apartment looks the same way it did during his interview except that it's dark outside. The pool glows ghostly blue out on the terrace.

"Do you swim?" I ask.

"All the time. It's something I've put a lot of effort into. I don't want to drown if I happen to fall off a boat."

I look up at him. "Is that something you worry about a lot?"

"It isn't something I worry about. I just don't want to make myself vulnerable to something happening just because I got hurt. It's kind of like if some lunatic moron attacks me on the street. I want to be able to defend myself just as well as if I was able-bodied. I don't see why I should disadvantage myself just because I got hit by a car. If I go on a boat, I want to be just as able to tread water and swim to shore as if I could still use my legs." He makes a face at me. "I work out a lot. Just warning you."

My eyes dip to his torso. "I can see that."

"Now you know why. It's important to me that I can still function, legs or no legs. People rely on their bodies being ready, willing, and able to perform when we need them to—but that isn't always the case. Something could happen. Someone could get hurt in a way that they wouldn't be able to use their legs to walk somewhere to deal with the situation. Then the person would need to use their arms to get where they need to go."

"I see what you mean. I can understand the motivation to stay on top of things. It's a smart way to look at it."

He rolls over to me, slips his hand into mine, and smiles up at me. "Do you want to go for a swim?"

I look away. "Maybe later."

"Come sit down."

He has to let go of my hand to push his wheelchair over to the couch. I sit down. He stays where he is and takes my hand again. He won't stop rubbing it. "What you said to me goes for you, too. You don't have to do anything if it's too hard."

"No...." I stammer. "I want to."

He doesn't say anything. He doesn't tell me to do whatever it is I say I want to do. I never dreamed it would be this hard. He's handling this so much better than I am.

He must sense that I'm freaking out big time. He doesn't make the first move. He just sits there holding my hand for a minute. Then he turns away and wheels his chair sideways. "Let's take a walk."

"Take a walk....here?" I look around. "Where?"

"We can go out on the terrace—or I could take you on a tour of the floor—whatever. It doesn't matter. Come on."

He crosses the room. I stand up to follow him. He stops at a side table, points a remote at the glass sliding doors leading to the terrace, and the doors slide open. He rolls out there and I follow him.

The light from the pool should make this a romantic setting—and it does. I look out at all the lighted windows in all the surrounding buildings.

Anyone looking out of one of those windows would be able to see us as easily as we can see them—but no one looks. We're completely alone out here.

"Do you remember what you said about all those windows being a different story?" he asks.

"Yes, I remember?"

"I've always thought the lights looked like constellations of stars in the night sky. My parents sent me to summer camp upstate when I was younger. The camp was way out in the middle of nowhere and it got really dark at night. You could see so many more stars. You could see the Milky Way as clear as anything. I'd never seen anything like that growing up in Queens. This always reminds me of that."

I get hypnotized by his voice and the view from the terrace. I forget all about what we're here for.

"I guess I was trying to recreate this with the Infection show," I tell him. "I guess I was trying to create something like this by showing all the little windows into other people's lives."

"It works. The pictures do show windows into other people's lives." He clasps my hand. "You're as good as Annie Leibowitz or maybe even better—and I should know. I've seen enough photography in my career."

I don't know what to say, but he turns aside again before I can contradict.

"Follow me," he tells me and leads me to the other side of the terrace. A wall separates the pool from another courtyard on the other side of the terrace. I didn't notice this before—and I guess that's kind of the point. The wall hides this area and makes it private.

The courtyard has been landscaped into a little miniature garden. Another sliding wall-door opens into a different room set up as an office and library.

A spiral ramp leads up to a second balcony above the terrace. I didn't realize this penthouse had multiple levels.

The spiral ramp would resemble a spiral staircase except that the ramp is much bigger. Its size makes the ramp not quite so steep. Giovanni wheels his wheelchair onto the ramp and pushes himself up it to the balcony.

The glass balustrade around the balcony opens in a swinging panel so he can get onto the balcony. I follow him and he pushes open another sliding glass wall to enter a giant bedroom.

Most of the space is empty with the huge bed set at a distance from the balcony door. The bedroom has a couch, coffee table, dresser, and another table and chair to one side.

The wall behind the bed separates the bedroom from a walk-through closet. One of the doors stands partially open so I can see Giovanni's clothes, shoes, and accessories inside.

The other side of the walk-through closet leads to the bathroom, but I can't see enough to tell how magnificent it is. I'm sure it's just as palatial as the rest of this place.

Chapter 14: Mila

Giovanni parks his wheelchair next to his bed. Everything in the bedroom is all on one level, too. He can get anywhere he wants to go whenever he wants to roll his chair somewhere.

He locks his wheels and uses his arms to push himself up and shift himself over to the bed. He sits down on the mattress, leans forward to unlock the wheels on his chair, and pushes it out of the way so it isn't near him.

I stop at a distance from him and regard him across the room. This is his bedroom. He brought me to his bedroom.

My heart hammers against my ribs. I don't know what to do with myself.

"Come here," he murmurs.

I take a few steps closer, but I just cannot summon the courage to go near enough to touch him.

He doesn't treat that as anything offensive or unusual.

"I understand you're nervous and maybe even terrified," he murmurs. "I meant what I said. You don't have to do anything. You can keep your clothes on and I won't lay a finger on you, but I want you to see. I want you to be the one who sees me as I really am. I only realized since I met you how badly I needed someone like you to see me and accept me. I need you to give me that even if you don't reciprocate."

I start to say, "I want to...." again, but he holds up his hand to stop me.

"Don't do anything," he breathes. "Just stand there."

I don't know what he means and I'm too nervous to ask.

He stares at me with a kind of intensity I don't understand. I've never seen him like this before. It isn't his smoldering passion look that he gets when he wants to tear my clothes off and ravage me like a wild animal. This is something else—something even bigger.

I stand frozen in nervous confusion—until he straightens up and starts pulling off his jacket. He throws it aside onto the bed next to him, yanks off his tie, and starts unbuttoning his shirt.

He never takes his eyes off me. His eyes challenge me not to look away. He's doing this. He's doing what he said. He wants me to see him. He didn't bring me here so he could chicken out. He doesn't care if I chicken out, but he won't.

His arms and chest muscles strain while he unbuttons his buttons. He pulls off his shirt and throws that on top of the jacket. He's wearing a beige T-shirt underneath his dress shirt. Now I have no choice but to see how jacked he really is.

He peels his T-shirt off. The ghostly light from the pool shines into the room and gives me all the light I need to see every detail of his body.

Scars crisscross his chest, arms, shoulders, and stomach. I don't know what caused them. He looks like he got attacked by a knife-wielding murderer.

He throws his T-shirt away, too, and bends over to untie his shoes. He pulls them off followed by his socks.

Things get real when he starts unbuckling his belt. He really plans to go all the way. He wants me to see everything.

He's the one who needs this. He needs it a hell of a lot more than I do—and he knows he needs it. He can't go any further without someone seeing—and I'm the one.

He pulls his fly open, hooks his thumbs into them and his boxer shorts, and angles his hips from side to side to scoot everything down over his hips.

He pushes his pants all the way down his legs and uses his hands to lift his feet out of his pants. He sets them aside and straightens up in front of me stark naked and sitting on the bed.

He actually doesn't look that different like this—except that he isn't wearing any clothes. He stares up at me with the same unwavering gaze of challenge and confrontation. He dares me to say one word to criticize him.

I could never criticize him—not for his body. He's magnificent. He's built like a god from the waist up. He's hands down the most muscular, defined, and powerful man I've ever seen—in person or in pictures.

He doesn't have a scrap of flesh on his leg bones. Below the hips he looks like something out of a POW camp or maybe a skeleton.

His feet stick out at the wrong angles and his swollen knees point the wrong way. His legs don't look like they belong to the same body.

"I want you to touch me," he murmurs. "I want you to touch me the way you talked about in the car. I want you to show me how attractive and appealing you think I am. I won't touch you back unless you want me to. Come here. You said you would show me so come here and show me."

I take a few steps closer. He's everything I dreamed he would be and more. He's so powerful like this. He isn't afraid of criticism or judgment. He isn't ashamed of who and what he is. He has no reason to be. He looks absolutely glorious.

His attitude shatters the spell. I want him to know how attractive and appealing he is. I want to give him that—and I want him. I crave him. He really is irresistible.

Giving me permission to touch him breaks the spell. I'm not afraid anymore—not of him, not of someone seeing my body—not of anything we could or would do in this room. Nothing we could or would do in this room could ever be wrong.

I stop in front of him, check within myself that I really do want this, and lift my dress to pull it over my head.

I drop it on top of his jacket and shirt. He stares up at me with so much earth-shattering intensity—and then his eyes trail downward to my body.

He can't see anything through my bra, but he can definitely see the giant chunk of flesh missing from my left leg. The skin rests right on top of the bone.

This is nothing he hasn't already seen in my picture from the Infection show. He won't see anything tonight that will surprise him.

I take a minute just to let him see me—and I see him. I can't do anything but see him sitting right there in front of me. I see every inch of his body. His chest hair starts at his sternum and angles downward into a dark arrow to his groin.

I lower myself onto my knees in front of him. I'm still wearing my bra and panties, but that will all go away very soon.

I'm not afraid of him criticizing or judging me, either. I'm not ashamed of anything he might see when he looks at me. I'm not keeping my bra and panties on to hide from him.

His eyes follow me down until I look at him from his level. I slide my hands onto his knees and up his thighs. They feel strange because they're so bony.

His breath catches when I get near his pelvis. I stroke his thighs in a light, teasing touch and he starts to get hard. He told the truth. He's perfectly functional and his anatomy is all as normal as any other man.

I push his thighs apart just a little bit—and then I dive in and bury my face in the side of his neck. I let go of all my inhibitions. I'm going to show him. I'm going to cover him in my body and fill him with more pleasure than he knows what to do with.

His breath rasps through gritted teeth as I crawl my mouth down his neck. He turns his head aside in an agonized, husky groan when I give him the gentlest nip on the neck and start working my way down his chest.

I suck his nipples and push him to lean back on his arms. His whole body strains when I get between his legs and tease him out of his mind.

His hand appears on my shoulder and he grips me tight in desperate, excruciating agony. I want him so damn bad. I want to feel and see and hear how much he needs this.

He needs a lot more than for me to see and touch him. He needs all of me—and that's what I plan to give him.

I work my mouth up and down his shaft to excite him even more. He gives a little gasp every time I spiral my lips around his sensitive head. He digs his fingers into my shoulder trying to cope with all the sensation coursing through him.

I wrap my arms around his hips to pull him into myself. I want to devour him and for him to devour me. I love feeling him like this. He tastes and feels as mouthwateringly intoxicating as I imagined.

I wrap my tongue around his nuts every time I take him into my throat. I let my fingers climb up his back to feel the rest of him tensing and shaking at my touch. I can't wait to explore all that he is.

He shifts his weight on the mattress without interrupting me. He can barely catch his breath in the frenzy of how much he wants this.

He unclips my bra and pulls it out of the way. He still can't see me when I'm bent over his lap like this.

He doesn't wait for me to do it for him. He scoops me under my armpits while I'm in mid-stroke, lifts me onto his lap to straddle him, and plunges his face into my breasts without giving me an instant to hesitate.

I scream when his mouth closes around my left breast—the one with part of it missing. He pays no attention to what it looks like or feels like. He crushes his whole face and mouth against it until it envelops his nose and mouth.

His hands won't stop clawing at me all over the place. He grabs my hips to pull me down on his hardness, but my panties get in the way.

I don't want to wait anymore. I didn't come here to chicken out, either, and his passion gives me the permission I need to go all the way.

I struggle against his powerful arms, pull my panties aside, and sit down on him. He roars into my chest when he feels his length plunge inside. I scream—and he pulls away to lock eyes with me.

He snarls at me in raving madness, seizes me, and thrusts me down on his shaft for all he's worth. I can't stop now. His eyes mesmerize me with what we're doing together.

He doesn't look at my leg or my breasts. He glares at me baring his teeth and his lips shiver every time he inhales.

I can't look away from that masterful stare. He holds me spellbound and compels my body to respond to him. I buck into him faster and feel the deep, satisfying thump of his iron filling me to the breaking point.

I spread my legs wider to take him all the way in. I need him so freakin' bad. I can't stop now.

His hand clamps on my breast and he squeezes to make me scream and toss in an agony of desire. I want to climax right now, but something's missing.

He acts so decisively. He gives me exactly what I need, scoops one arm behind my waist, and flips me over on the bed. He rolls sideways at the same time and stays between my legs when he rotates on top of me

.

He buries his hips between my legs, braces himself up on his arms, and uses all his stomach muscles to crunch inward to hammer my legs apart.

I scream as each earth-shattering concussion blasts me apart. I writhe on the bed in front of him as exposed and unguarded as I was in the picture. He can see my whole body laid out for him here.

He roars with every thrust and screws his hips in tight at his deepest point to drive me farther up the bed. I can't hold back. I dissolve in screaming climax right in front of him. I can't spread my legs wide enough to take him deep enough to satisfy myself.

His useless legs lie down the bed behind him. He doesn't think about them or mention them. They disappear as though they were never there.

His eyes consume my heart and soul. His granite body conquers me in all its power and leaves me fragile and aching for more as soon as it's over.

I want to crawl over onto my side and hide from how excruciatingly incredible this feels, but he isn't finished with me. He pulls off, supports his weight on one arm, and lifts my right leg to roll me onto my stomach.

I don't know what I expect him to do. My brain shuts down in the dizzy insanity of what he's doing to me.

He flops on the bed behind me, turns onto his back, and crawls between my legs from below. He wraps his arms around my hips and pulls my trembling flesh down on top of his face.

I scream again when his hot, electric tongue touches my swollen flesh, but he's not about to let me go. He holds me in position and lights me on fire all over again until I need him enough to ride down on his face.

I try to sit up and he finally loosens his arms enough to let me. I arch my hips into his mouth until he impales me with two fingers and sends me blasting into another broken, screaming release.

I can't stand this. I'm too sensitive to function right now. I crawl off him onto the bed, but I should know better than to think he'll just let me run away.

He pivots onto his stomach, grabs me by the ankle, and pulls me back down the bed toward him. I expect him to attack me from behind, but he doesn't.

He pushes himself up on his arms and uses them to drag himself up the bed. He can move around perfectly well this way. His legs don't slow him down at all.

He turns me onto my side, dives down to my level, and starts kissing me to the ends of the earth. His haunted eyes hover right in front of me. He sees exactly what he's doing to me and he wants more of it.

He doesn't look away from my devastation. He knows he's the cause and the cure all in one.

I can't turn aside when he kisses me like that. I want to cry from the look of pure love and admiration in those eyes. He sees me. He respects me as much now as he did before we did it. He cares for me, protects me, and elevates me even as he takes me for his own.

I wrap my arms around his neck kissing him back just as hard. I need him more now than I did before.

He lowers himself onto the bed next to me, pulls me toward him, and lifts one of my legs over his elbow so he can drill into me from that angle.

I can't stop staring into those eyes. He never flinches. He never hesitates.

He sees me and I see him—and yet neither of us sees whatever might be wrong with our bodies. I don't see his legs right now. His legs are the absolute last thing on my mind.

He doesn't see my leg or my breast, either. He doesn't care about any of that. He sees what's in my heart reflected through my eyes. He sees all my aching need for him pouring out through my eyes and into his.

His eyes tell me more than I ever needed to know about who and what he is—and how much he respects and admires me. He could never treat me like a piece of meat or a superficial one-night roll in the hay. It could never be like that between us.

"You're so beautiful," he murmurs.

I want to sob. "I need you!" I choke. "I need you so bad!"

"You have me. Don't you see how much you have me? There's no one else. You're the only one."

Chapter 15: Giovanni

I startle out of a sound sleep when I realize someone is in my bed. I've studiously avoided sleeping with any other person for my entire life. The idea of someone in my bed is probably my worst fear in life.

That fear got so much worse after the accident. I became irrationally terrified that someone would see me naked while I was asleep. I worried about that all the time even when I slept in pajamas.

I collapse in relief when I see Mila sprawled naked on the bed next to me. Thank goodness it's her. I couldn't stand it if it was anyone else.

I don't have to worry about her seeing me because she already did. She lays at a crooked angle where I can finally see her leg and breast in the sunlight coming through the window. They don't look that different from her Infection picture.

That's the thing about her photography. She doesn't use fancy tricks to make the person's body look better than it is. She actually uses the camera to make the flaw—or supposed flaw—look as starkly realistic as possible.

She coordinates every other detail of the picture to showcase the person's inner beauty. She lies on my bed in exactly the same position she photographed herself except that now her eyes are closed.

Her hair sprays across my bed in a glorious sheet of brilliant copper. The sunshine highlights all the red tints and shimmers on all the peach fuzz on her skin.

Her whole being glows with sex, vitality, and angelic beauty. I can only lie here and bask in the radiance of her perfection.

I know she sees me the same way because she looked at me like that last night. She feasted her eyes on me—and her mouth and body. She bathed me in it beyond anything I could have imagined. She's everything I dreamed she would be.

She doesn't hold back from letting me see how much she needs and craves me. She doesn't guard herself or turn all of this into a meaningless game. It means something. It means a lot and that's exactly what she wants.

That's what I want, too. I want it to mean everything. I want everything she is and for her to take everything that I want to give her. I don't want to hold anything back from her.

I'm just starting to drift back to sleep in the exhaustion from last night when she stirs. She whimpers, twists onto her side, and her hair covers her face before she crawls back into my arms. She feels magical like this.

She huddles in my arms, buries her face in my chest, and crashes out again. So do I.

I wake up when I hear the toilet flush in the other room. She comes back in with her hair all over the place and her face puffy and blotchy from sleep. She grumbles under her breath, scoots under the covers, and curls up next to me all soft and warm.

"Don't you have anything you want to do today?" I murmur into her hair.

She doesn't answer right away. I think she might have fallen back to sleep, but she eases back, rests her head on my bicep, and drags her hazy eyes open to study me. "Can I ask you a question?"

"Of course," I tell her. "Anything you want."

"How would you feel about me photographing you now."

I shrug that away. "Okay. I could do that." I frown. "Why do you want to? You know what I look like."

"I know what you look like, but I don't think *you* know what you look like."

I frown. "I don't understand. Of course I know what I look like."

"I don't think so. I think you would see something in the pictures that you don't see when you look at yourself in the mirror every day."

I turn my head to look away. I have no doubt she would see something in me that I don't see when I look at myself in the mirror every day. That's what all her Infection pictures are. They show the person's inner beauty in ways they can't see for themselves.

I change the subject. "I have to make a few phone calls later. You should feel free to stick around as long as you want to unless you have any prior commitments."

"What are the phone calls about? We don't have to spend the day together if you have to work."

"These phone calls aren't work-related. I have to call Kevin Drake about the next club gala."

"Are you one of the organizers?"

"Hell no! I don't get involved with all of that."

"Why not? Someone has to do it."

"Someone does do it. Someone much better qualified does it. I'm no good at any of that."

"Something tells me you would be good at just about anything if you really set your mind to it."

"Anyway, I already RSVPed for the gala and told him I was coming alone—so I have to change that to let him know I'm bringing a plus-one."

She giggles. "That sounds official."

"It is. It's a formal affair, so I want to take you shopping and buy you a new dress for the occasion." I roll in her direction and run my fingers through her hair so I can admire how gorgeous she is. "I want you to have the best."

She smiles at me and her features soften when she sees me looking at her like that. "Why did you decide to go alone?"

I shrug. "I always took hired girls before—or just anyone who happened to be throwing themselves at me at the time. I don't do that since the accident. I haven't taken anyone to a gala since then."

"I don't know," she murmurs. "I don't know if I'm good-looking enough to compete with a bunch of billionaires and their wives and girlfriends."

"It has nothing to do with who's good-looking enough. It isn't a beauty pageant. Anyway, the billionaires and their wives and girlfriends aren't trying to compete against whatever hired girls the young studs bring as their dates. The billionaires and their wives and girlfriends are there to enjoy each other's company in a social setting. The people who really matter don't care what a person looks like. They all like each other and support each other too much to turn it into that."

She stares at me with wide eyes. "That sounds amazing."

"It would be if I had someone who was like that—and if I was a decent enough person to be a part of it."

"I'm sure you are."

"Maybe I will be if I keep going the way I am. I'm not there yet."

"So....what happens? Do they not even talk to you or something?"

"It's more that I didn't talk to them. I was too busy competing against the young studs and thinking about if my hired girl was hotter than their hired girl."

She laughs at me. "What a slut you were."

"You have no idea."

She won't stop giggling. "What did the older married billionaires think of that?"

"They were much more forgiving about it than I am turning out to be. It's a miracle they even continued to do business with me considering the way I acted."

"So what will they think when they find out you're seeing someone?"

"I'm sure they'll be thrilled. They would love it if I pulled my head out of my ass, settled down, and became one of them."

She beams at me. "You really need to stop being so hard on yourself."

"I guess the problem was that I was petrified of sliding back into becoming that again. It would have been easy to use my money to hire a different girl every night to come up here and service me like I might hire a technician to service my computer."

"Giovanni!" she exclaims. "Stop talking about yourself like that."

"I'm just saying I could have. I didn't. I didn't want to become that. I was worried the accident would make me into that—or that I would continue to be the worthless, shallow slut I was before. I'm not worried about it now—not now that I have you."

She surprises me by rolling on top of me. She pushes me down on my back and stretches her silky body all over me. She feels luscious.

She straddles her legs over me and starts rubbing her wet slit over me to tease me hard again. She kisses me with her eyes open and rocks her body to caress her breasts up and down my chest.

"Will you let me be your computer technician?" she asks between kisses. "I'll service you."

"How do you know I'm not the one serving you?" I grab her hips to pull her into me and then my hand closes on her breast.

Her left breast feels odd because it has so little tissue compared to a normal breast. The nipple still feels normal, though. I pinch it and massage the rest of her breast to make her grimace and squeal.

I try to maneuver my body between her legs, but she winds up doing it herself in the end. She moans and spirals her hips to drive me wild. Her sweet honey gushes all over me as she winds up to another delirious climax.

She's been climaxing all night long. I don't know how she can keep going like this, but she always does. She's insatiable.

She kisses me long and deep. Her pathetic little whimpers of pleasure and desire thrill me to the core. I love making her sob like that and then scream when she completely ruptures in the throes of ecstasy.

She sits all the way up and smiles down at me while she rides me to the ends of the earth. I can never get enough of seeing her like this. Her breasts fall into my hands and she digs her fingertips into my chest as her expression goes dark and serious.

She throws back her head, slams her juicy flesh down on top of me, and shrieks when I bump up into her from below. She makes me so damn hard that I can't stand it, but I always hold back and try to wait as long as possible so I can see her like this just a little longer.

She collapses across me still whining and quivering as the convulsions subside. Now she's all mine. I roll her onto her back, pivot between her legs, and push myself up on my arms.

I love seeing her like this, too. Every position gives me some new sense of her delights. I like this one best for eye contact. She floats there below me surrounded in a halo of pure rapture.

She understands exactly what I need from her in this moment. Her eyes float open to stare up at me.

She looks the way she did in her Infection picture. I can imagine her like that—displayed for my pleasure like a goddess and I'm the hero who gets to ravage her and taste her divine nectar.

Her hair scatters around her head and she raises her arms so I can see her body tremble at every thrust. Her flesh belongs to me, but it's her pure heart that I want most.

Her lips shiver when she rasps for breath. Her eyes keep blurring out of focus and her breasts sway in my face until I plunge in and devour them. She cries out when I do that.

She spreads her legs to welcome me in and I fall head over heels into her dark bliss. I try again to hold back, but she's so beautiful and succulent that I wind up escalating to another explosion.

I keep expecting both of us to collapse in exhaustion, but her endless desire keeps me going. I don't want to miss any of it. I want to find out how far it really goes and if and when she'll ever tell me to stop. I can't imagine her ever doing that.

I lower myself on top of her feeling both of our juices bubbling around my shaft and running down her ass and thighs. I sink into lying on top of her and holding her while we kiss for the ages.

She hugs me down on top of her still rocking her hips on me until I go soft again. I could drift off into sleep again. I shouldn't. I should get up and go do something productive.

I roll onto my side, but I just can't bring myself to get out from between her legs. I want to stay here forever.

I've never felt this for anyone before. I never wanted any of my previous girls to stick around after the fact and I sure as hell never wanted to have any conversations with them after the fact. I wanted them to disappear—or for me to disappear.

I can't do that with her and I don't want to. The conversations we have are somehow even more enjoyable than the sex. The sex is just foreplay to the conversations where we explore each other's hearts and minds in new and unforeseen ways.

I finally go soft enough that I have no more reason to stay between her legs. My weight traps one of her legs underneath me and makes us both uncomfortable, so I shift position so we can both lie down.

We're in the middle of that when my phone rings in my pants pocket. My pants still lie on the floor by the foot of the bed where I left them last night.

I crawl out of bed to go get it. Mila smacks my ass and giggles when I bend over with my ass pointing in her direction.

"You are going to be in so much trouble as soon as I finish this," I mutter over my shoulder.

She only snickers again, slips her hand between my legs, and grabs me around the nuts. I freeze when I feel her holding me like that, but she massages them extra gently. No one has ever played with me like this before.

I have to concentrate hard to send Kevin a text about bringing a date to the gala after all. He's more than happy to oblige. Then I look up the Annie Leibowitz Award for Excellence in Photography.

The awards ceremony is another formal gala event. I mark the date on my calendar and rearrange a few other non-essential tasks so I can be there for Mila.

She plays with me for as long as I stay in that position. I take my phone with me when I lie back down so I can do what I need to do and have the rest of the day off to enjoy with her.

She watches me tap on my phone for a few minutes. My head is somewhere completely different when she sits up, throws off the covers, and crawls down there between my legs.

I gasp when she sucks me into her mouth and starts driving me into outer space again. I try to pull her away, but she feels too good. My hand automatically flies to her head. It's like this every time she sucks me. She breaks down every barrier so I can't stop what's happening.

Her mouth intoxicates me. I try to hold back, but she eventually sends me reeling off into the stratosphere of another crushing release.

She sprawls back on the bed all soft and undulating with sex. She's irresistible like this. I don't even know if I can get hard again. I'm too drained and exhausted, so I roll her over and crawl between her legs instead.

I can get lost down here and make her scream in ecstasy for the rest of the day if I have to. I can think of worse ways to spend the next twenty-four hours.

Chapter 16: Mila

I hover on the edge between being asleep and awake. I float in some watery half-dreams for a while and roll onto my side to put my arms around Giovanni. Sleeping with him is so peaceful and comforting.

I love drifting awake, wrapping my arms around him, and drifting straight off again knowing that he's right here next to me.

I love it when he wakes up and rolls on top of me to do it with me when we're both still mostly asleep. We do it in our dreams. Doing it with him feels instinctive. It feels like an automatic body process like breathing or digestion.

I want to nuzzle into him and feel how big and hard and strong he is. His strength and hardness make me softer. He makes me melt and liquify before his hardness. I want to feel that way. I want to feel myself ooze around his hardness.

I don't put my arms around him.....because he isn't here. The other side of the bed is empty. I have to wake up fully before I understand that he isn't here.

I push myself up on my elbow and look around the bedroom. He isn't here. He isn't anywhere in the bedroom. I don't see him at all.

I sit all the way up trying to think where he would be. His wheelchair is gone, so he must have left the room. Where could he be? I have no idea even where to begin to look. I stand up and glance into the closet, but of course he isn't in there.

I have nothing to wear except my dress from our date the other night. His bathrobe hangs from the hook behind the closet door, but I don't want to wear that or anything else of his—not without asking. We aren't there yet.

I slip back into my bra and panties and pull the dress over my head. I stick my head out the bedroom door and find myself looking down a hallway toward another spiral ramp. It leads down to the main penthouse living room.

The apartment entrance door stands open to the hall outside. I go out there and hear thumping noises coming from a different open door farther down the hall. I don't want to accidentally walk in on Andy doing anything I shouldn't see.

Both doors are open, so I guess I'm safe for now. I go down there and stand in the hall staring in.

This has to be Giovanni's home gym. A giant weight rack occupies one side of the big room.

The other half of the room has an enormous jungle gym of interconnected metal pipes in different configurations. Ladders climb up to a scaffold of monkey bars and gymnastic rings.

Giovanni doesn't work out on the scaffold—not right now. He hangs from a different structure attached to the wall. This is a giant wooden board drilled full of holes.

He wears a pair of sweatpants and nothing else. He holds two wooden pegs in his hands, pulls himself up and across the board, and anchors himself by sticking the pegs into the holes before he pulls himself to the next position.

He crawls up, down, and back and forth across the board with fast, practiced movements. All the muscles of his broad back and shoulders strain from the effort, but he does each move easily and in perfect control.

Sweat trickles down his body and saturates his hair, but he barely gets out of breath. He takes little gasping breaths through his nose every time he pulls himself to a new level where he can move his pegs somewhere else.

His useless legs dangle below him. He doesn't do anything to restrain them or keep them from interfering with his movements.

He works himself closer to the floor and sideways to another side of the board where much larger holes cover a different section of wooden boards. He leaves the pegs there and transfers to these larger holes that he holds onto with his bare hands.

He goes through the same process of pulling himself up, climbing all over the wall in every direction, and eventually travels around to the scaffold of pipes. He holds onto the wooden wall with one hand, grabs one of the pipes, and continues moving all over it.

He climbs the pipes hand over hand, works down the monkey bars and up and down the ladders, does a whole bunch of muscle-ups, and eventually swings over to the rings where he does a modified gymnastics workout.

He can't do some of the more complicated moves that involve the legs, but he can do an Iron Cross and he does muscle-ups on the rings before he swings himself back over to the scaffold.

He uses the pipes to carry himself back to his wheelchair which stands there waiting for him at the bottom of one of the ladders. He lowers himself into the seat, positions his feet on the rests, and unlocks the wheels before he notices me standing there.

"Oh, hello," he remarks. "I thought you were asleep."

"I was. I didn't know where you were." I look around at his gym. "This is amazing."

"It's like I told you. I like to be prepared in case anything happens." He rolls to the other side of the room, takes a towel off the weight bench, and rubs the sweat off his face and neck.

"Was this place like this when you bought it?" I ask.

"No, it was just a weight room. I don't know what the previous owner's disability was, but he had a lot of leg equipment that I don't need. I got rid of all of that and put in all of *that.*" He nods toward the scaffold and the wooden wall. "None of that was here before." He grins at me. "Do you want to get in a workout?"

I can't even take the joke. "I would definitely have to work up to it before I could do anything like that."

He rolls his chair toward the door. "I'm going to go do my swim. Do you want to come?"

I follow him out of the room. "What do you think about doing your photoshoot today—if you aren't too busy?"

"We could do it today—as long as we can do it here."

"Sure. Of course. I'll need to go get my equipment from my apartment."

"I can text Andy to drive you over there while I get my phone calls and business out of the way. Then I'll be able to give you my undivided attention. Just don't do the photoshoot when I look like this."

I stare down at him sitting bare-chested in his wheelchair. "You look amazing like this."

He blushes and laughs. "I'm glad you think so."

He rolls out to the living room, opens the sliding glass wall, and stops his chair next to a picnic table on the terrace. A stack of clothes sits there waiting for him and he starts changing into a full suit, tie, jacket, belt, shoes, and even adds the T-shirt underneath.

"What are you doing?" I ask. "You said you were going swimming."

"I am going swimming. I do my swimming workout fully clothes. I told you before. I swim like this so I would be ready to save my own life if I fell off a boat. I wouldn't likely fall off a boat in my swimming trunks, would I?"

I eye his suit. It isn't his usual impeccable Tom Ford. The suit shows the unmistakable signs of chlorine stains.

He catches me looking at it. "I don't want to wreck one of my good suits. This is my real swimsuit."

He laughs at his own joke, but I can't. I can't believe he takes this so seriously. I shouldn't be surprised, but I am. I guess I'm just surprised that he's such an amazing, driven, motivated person—even more than I realized he was.

He drapes his towel over the back of his seat, steers his wheelchair to the other end of the swimming lane, sets the brakes, and takes his feet off the rests. Then he leans all the way over and lets his weight topple out of the chair onto the pavement.

He lands on his hands in a push-up position with his legs crumpled underneath him.

He uses his arms to hitch himself over to the pool, rolls over to sit up, and then uses his hands to swing his legs into the water. I've seen him do stuff like this ever since I came home with him. He moves around in bed like this. It all comes naturally to him.

He lowers himself into the lane, plunges to dunk his head, and starts swimming laps. His own strength and speed pulls his legs out behind him. They trial along back there, but they don't slow him down—or he doesn't let them.

He doesn't let the suit slow him down, either. He has to pull against the drag, but he strokes hard and fast swimming lap after lap. He goes on for a long time. I don't know what time limit he puts on it or if he swims a certain distance every time.

He eventually stops at the far end of the pool next to his chair, muscles himself up onto the pavement, and flips himself around to sit on the edge of the pool.

Water pours from his suit and even runs out of his shoes. He doesn't care if he wrecks these clothes by soaking them in chlorinated water.

He finally strips off his clothes and shoes, grabs his towel, dries himself off, and hauls himself all dry and naked back into his wheelchair.

He hangs his clothes over the deck chairs to dry and cracks another blushing grin when he sees me watching him. "Is this like going to the zoo?"

"Definitely. I'm pretty sure you're the only person on Planet Earth who does it this way."

He laughs. "I'm sure I am—and let's keep it that way."

"How do you train for self-defense?" I ask. "Do you have a trainer or something?"

"I go to an MMA gym where I study boxing and grappling. I actually study kickboxing even though I don't do any kicking—but it's a form of upper body fighting that uses more elbows and palm strikes than traditional boxing. I have a coach who helps me modify different fighting styles to my situation. So I pick and choose different techniques and combine them into a style that works for me."

"That's amazing."

"Why do you keep saying that? I'm not going to let myself slide away into an early grave at my age. I have to stay healthy somehow. I might as well stay active and prepared while I'm at it. It isn't my fault I got hit by a car. I'm not going to throw my life away because of it."

"I'm just saying it's impressive that you do all of this to compensate for not being able to use your legs. I can't think of anyone else who would go to such lengths."

He ignores that and pulls his chair away. "Come upstairs with me while I change. I'll call Andy and tell him you want to go over to your apartment to get your stuff."

Chapter 17: Mila

I follow Giovanni up the spiral ramp to his bedroom. He rolls around everywhere doing everything. He goes into his closet, picks out a set of casual clothes he wants to wear today, and moves himself over to the bed to change.

He gets dressed in the reverse order that he took off his clothes last night. He bends over to pull his pants over his feet, hitches his hips from side to side to scoot his pants around his waist, buckles his belt, puts on his socks and shoes, and then pulls his T-shirt over his head.

He buttons his dress shirt and straightens all his clothes in front of the closet mirror. Then he combs and gels his hair so he's ready for the rest of the day.

He comes out of the closet and sees me watching him. "Why is it so fascinating to you?"

"Do you mean the process of watching a paralyzed person get dressed? That isn't what's fascinating to me. You are."

He blushes and looks away. "I'm sure I'm just an ordinary guy like any other."

"That's what's fascinating about it. You're an ordinary guy living an ordinary life. You just do things your own way that works for you. It's interesting to see how you do everything and how you've modified your whole life so you can keep doing what you want to do and thriving. It's admirable."

"I'm sure it isn't as admirable as what you're doing. I won't be changing anyone's life by doing my workouts, getting dressed, and running my business."

"You're changing my life," I tell him. "Doesn't that count?"

He looks up and pulls me in to kiss me. "If I can give you anything of value, then I would say all of this has been worth it. Come downstairs. Andy is on his way over to pick you up."

We go downstairs just as Andy strolls into Giovanni's apartment. Giovanni leaves the door open so Andy doesn't have to knock.

Giovanni rubs my hand before I leave. "Bring some extra clothes back with you so you can spend the night tonight."

I raise my eyebrows. "Really?"

"Stay as long as you want. Stay forever."

I kiss him. "I'll be back as soon as I can."

I walk out with Andy and we get into the elevator. He keeps smiling at me every time I catch his eye.

"You make him very happy," Andy tells me.

I look away. "That makes two of us, doesn't it?"

"You two are perfect for each other."

I can't help but look up at him. "How long have you worked for him?"

He shrugs. "Only since he came home from the hospital. He drove his own cars before that. He hired limos when he wanted to ride in a limo. I drove for a hire service before and I drove him a few times. That's how we knew each other, but I didn't work for him full-time like I do now. He contacted me after he got out of the hospital and made me an offer I couldn't refuse."

He laughs at his joke.

"So....did you know what he was like before?" I ask.

"Oh, yeah. All the limo drivers knew about him. He was notorious. Limos were his thing. He didn't often make it back to his place—not with the girl or girls. He would do them in the limo, drop them somewhere afterward, and then go home alone."

I face front. I don't want to hear about that and I don't need to hear about it. It's the same thing Giovanni has already told me.

"You're a very special young lady," Andy tells me. "And he cares for you very much."

We don't talk any more until I get down to the parking garage. Andy sticks his head into the passenger compartment and moves the sliding board down to the floor.

He props it in front of and against the seat so I can get in and sit down. Then he drives me back to my apartment. Riding in the limo feels strange without Giovanni here.

Andy gets out and opens the door for me. "Mr. Nowaczyk asked me to go upstairs with you and help you bring down any of your equipment you needed help with."

"That won't be necessary. I can carry it all and I want to take a shower, change my clothes, and pack a few other things. You can wait down here."

"Whatever you want. Let me give you my number in case you change your mind and want to call me to help you."

I frown at him. "Really? Are you okay with that? Are you sure Giovanni is okay with that?"

Andy makes a face at me. "Something tells me I'm going to be driving you around for a while. Just take my number in case you need me. I wouldn't want anything to happen to you while we were out and about together. I'm responsible for you when Mr. Nowaczyk isn't around."

I put my head down and pull out my phone. I don't know what to think about Andy and Giovanni conspiring....to what? To keep me safe? Why would I have a problem with that?

Andy and I exchange numbers and I go upstairs. I take a shower, change into a casual outfit, and pack an overnight bag. I don't know how long I'll stay at Giovanni's. What if it does turn into forever? Would I have a problem with that—and why would I?

I finally gather up my camera gear and laptop, take everything downstairs to the car, and Andy drives me back to Giovanni's penthouse.

"Great! You're just in time," Giovanni tells me. "I just finished."

"Not so fast, hotshot. I have to get set up first." I look around the apartment. "Where do you want to do it?"

He frowns at me. "What do you mean? What are the options?"

"Well, you've seen the other Infection pictures. You could do it sitting down, lying down, standing up....."

He bursts out laughing. "You're the photographer here. Just put me where you want me."

I find myself studying him. I can think of a lot of places and poses I could use to showcase how impressive he is, both inside and out. I decide to take him out by the pool.

I tell him to sit on the edge of the pool where he was when he first got into the lap lane. "Take your clothes off, jump in, and get water all over yourself," I tell him.

He won't stop laughing at me. "I just did my hair. Now you're gonna make me have to do it all over again."

"You don't have to get your hair wet. Just make it look like you just got out of the pool after your swim."

He strips off, lowers himself into the water up to his neck, and pulls himself back up to sit on the edge of the pavement.

"That's perfect." I raise my camera. "Now lean back and prop yourself on your arms."

He does it—and then he levels me with a hard look across the corner of the pool. I have to squat there since I can't get right in front of him.

His eyes challenge me and the viewer to find any fault in him. There isn't any fault to find.

The sunshine glitters on all the beads of water all over his body. This position makes him look powerful, mesmerizing, and unbelievably hot. His legs fall slightly apart. He looks like any normal, able-bodied man sitting on the edge of the pool.

The sun reflects off the pool water to shine on his face. The light gives him a haunted, smoldering look. I brought all my lighting equipment from my apartment, but I wind up not needing any of it. The light coming from the pool is perfect.

I snap a bunch of frames of him in that position. Then I get him to dry off, go into the living room, and recline on the couch with one arm thrown over the couch cushions behind him.

He looks like a supermodel like this. His face and body draw the viewer's eyes to how stunningly attractive he is. His legs don't seem to enter the picture at all.

Then I take him back to his gym where I take a bunch of pictures of him doing pull-ups and muscle-ups on his scaffold.

The same thing happens. His face and upper body command so much attention that the pictures come out hardly registering either that he's naked or that his legs don't match up with the rest of him.

"Now what?" he asks after I tell him he can get dressed.

"Now I have to process the pictures on my computer." I open my laptop on the living room coffee table. "This won't take long. Then you can see the pictures and tell me which one you want to use in the show."

He frowns at me. "You let the subject choose?"

"Of course. The picture is supposed to represent you. I wouldn't want to use a picture you didn't like or that you didn't think was the best image of yourself."

He shrugs that off and I get to work. I adjust the brightness, contrast, and palette tone of some of the pictures, but most of them are perfect the way they are.

I create a slideshow on my computer and take it over to the couch to show him the finished product. He pulls his wheelchair over to me so we can both see the screen.

He goes quiet and scowls at the pictures while I roll through them. He doesn't say anything until I get to the end. Then he pulls his chair away, rolls over to the windows, and stares out them in silence for a long time.

"Do you like them?" I ask after a minute.

"Yes," he murmurs.

I wait, but he doesn't turn around. "Are you okay? I only meant for you to see how attractive and appealing you are—like we agreed last night."

He doesn't answer for a long time. He sits there with his back to me. "You're right," he finally murmurs. "I didn't see it before, but I do now."

"Does it help?" I ask.

He barely speaks above a whisper. "Yes. It helps."

I don't know what to think or say. He doesn't act like he likes the pictures at all. I think he looks incredible. He does look incredible.

"Which one would you like to use in the show?" I ask.

He turns his chair around, comes over to me, and uses the arrow buttons to navigate back to the pictures by the pool. He points to one of the images of himself with the pool light reflecting on his face. "That one."

"I like that one the best, too," I tell him.

He doesn't answer. He pulls his chair away, goes into the kitchen, and starts making lunch. We skipped breakfast somewhere along the way.

He works in silence and we eat in silence. I can't tell if anything is wrong with him or what he has on his mind, but it must be something pretty serious.

Maybe now he's starting to realize that he's so much more than he realized. Maybe now he'll start to see himself the way I see him.

Chapter 18: Giovanni

I shoot Mila a grin in the back of the limo. We sit holding hands on our way to the Annie Leibowitz Awards. Mila wears a brand-new, stunning couture black off-the-shoulder gown that makes her look exquisite.

She radiates beauty and charm. She's so much more beautiful than any girl I've ever taken to any event in my life. She makes me so unbelievably happy.

The pictures she took of me are starting to work their magic on me. They make me see that I'm not actually a cripple at all.

I only saw those pictures once, but I'll never be able to forget them. I look unbelievable in them. I never would have guessed I could look like that. She's right. She sees something in me that I didn't see in myself.

I only realize after seeing them how much I've been holding myself back. I told myself I wouldn't let the accident slow me down or stop me, but I did let it. I let it slow me down and stop me a lot.

I assumed that the rest of the world saw me as crippled, disabled, disadvantaged, and weakened. I assumed my disability meant I was somehow less than the person I used to be.

Now I realize how wrong I was. I'm not less than the person I used to be. I'm much more than the person I used to be.

I never could have become the person I see in those pictures if not for the accident. I'm stronger, both physically and mentally. I'm bigger and more powerful, both mentally and physically. I'm everything I ever could have wanted to be and so much more.

I actually feel like I'm worthy of Mila's care and affection when I see myself as that. I'm good enough, strong enough, and mature enough to be the man in her life.

I never would have believed that if I hadn't seen those pictures. Some part of me would always continue to doubt if I would ever be good enough or if she was settling for less than she deserved.

Now I know I deserve her. I can be the man she needs me to be. I *am* the man she needs me to be. She gave me that.

She's been staying at my apartment for the past month. I never want her to leave, but we haven't had that conversation yet.

The limo pulls up in front of the venue. The awards ceremony is being held at Koch Hall at Lincoln Center. Andy gets out at Robertson Plaza and sets up my wheelchair. We aren't close enough to the hall for anyone to see us yet.

Mila squints across the plaza and Revson Fountain at the building in the distance. "I don't know about this...."

"Just stay near me," I tell her. "I'll protect you from them."

She laughs. "Thank God for that."

I settle into my chair and she rests her hand on my shoulder on our way across the plaza. Andy drives off in the limo.

More and more people in eveningwear gather around the building as we get closer. Mila's nerves start to escalate.

"Nothing to worry about," I murmur to her. "You're the star of the show here. Everyone here admires your work. They're here to honor you. You don't have to worry about anyone thinking the wrong thing or looking down on you."

"I'm just not used to this...." Her voice squeaks.

I want to hold her hand, but I have to use my arms to wheel myself forward. We get close to the entrance, but I can't get up the steps. She breaks away and asks one of the organizers where we can find a wheelchair-accessible entrance.

The woman leads us to the back of the building, down a long cargo hallway, and we get into an elevator that takes us to the lobby.

We walk into a crowd of hundreds of people all dressed up in their finest. Mila rests her hand on my shoulder again and we glide out into the throng.

People recognize her and come over to congratulate her. Voices fly in all directions. She looks absolutely breathtaking smiling at everyone and blushing when they compliment her.

A bunch of people shake my hand and exclaim in surprise when they realize I'm here as Mila's date. I couldn't be prouder of her.

We finally file into the hall. The organizers direct her to a special box of seats in the middle of the hall. We have to take the elevator up there again. Now everyone can see me sitting next to her.

The awards ceremony starts with a bunch of people giving speeches. First the founder of the endowment gives a speech about Annie Leibowitz, how influential she was, and how the award is intended to continue her legacy by honoring photographers that use the art to make as big a social impact as she did.

Then a few different people give speeches about the Infection Project, how important it is, and the massive benefit the project has had on so many people's lives.

Two of the presenters are in the Infection show. They tell their personal stories of how Mila's photography gave them their lives, their bodies, and their confidence back.

One man even credits the process with saving his marriage, his family, and bringing him back from the brink of suicide.

A bunch of people in the crowd wipe away tears while these people talk. Everyone applauds the stories and then the president of the endowment stands up to present the award to Mila.

She goes down to the stage to accept it and then approaches the microphone to give her remarks.

"Thank you all for your kind words and generous recognition. I wouldn't have been able to complete this project if not for the courage and support of all the subjects involved in the show and even more people who gave anonymous interviews. One thing I've learned from this process is that all of us feel the same way and secretly harbor these doubts, insecurities, and shame in our hearts. We all think we're hiding something that no one else would be able to tolerate looking at or acknowledging, but the truth is that everyone we see and know is going through exactly the same thing. Each of the interviewees—each quote you see on the gallery wall—these people are expressing the words that each of us is thinking and trying to hide from those around us. I started this project as a way to heal myself and somehow get over the shame of thinking I was disgusting and unlovable. These pictures helped me to see that I'm as human as everyone else—and as such, I'm as beautiful as everyone else. If one of us is ugly, all of us are ugly. If one of us is beautiful, all of us are beautiful. The truth is that beauty and ugliness can never be about what's on the outside. If we see someone as beautiful, it's because of the person they are on the inside. If we get to know someone and they're a terrible person who hurts others and uses them for personal gain, we'll see the person as ugly no matter what the person looks like on the outside. Those first impressions that make us think a person is really hot—they never last. The minute the person opens their mouth or we see them acting a certain way, they'll become horribly, hideously ugly to us—and the same is also true for a good person. It doesn't matter if someone is deformed or ugly or scarred. We'll see them as beautiful and incredibly attractive as soon as we see them being kind, considerate, and loving toward others. I'm grateful to all of you for the recognition you've given this project, but the truth is that this award belongs to everyone who took part in the project, everyone who bared their hearts and let me see what wonderful, beautiful, powerful people they are, and everyone who let me show that to the rest of the world. Thank you."

The hall erupts in cheers when she raises the award, bows the crowd, waves, and returns to her seat. She flushes with pride and relief when she catches my eye. She said those words for me as much as for everyone else.

I love the way she connected my past with my present. I was ugly before. I was hideous, disgusting, and no one could tolerate being around me.

Now I'm handsome—or I'm getting there. I'm earning that by being the man I'm supposed to be. I'm being a good man, treating her right, and growing into someone who might actually be able to do some good in the world.

The applause goes on for a long time. Everyone turns to watch her sit down. They all see her sitting next to me. Now the whole world knows we're together.

I clasp her hand. She's brilliant and gorgeous, but her real beauty comes from being a good person who genuinely wants to help people.

We get through a few other speeches about the award, the endowment, and a few other pieces of business, but the ceremony is all but over. Everyone pours out into the lobby, rubs elbow, sips champagne, and talks for another hour before it's time to go home.

I text Andy to come and pick us up. Mila takes a long time to say goodbye to everyone, thank them for everything, and then she thanks the organizers and the endowment board.

We finally walk outside into the night air. She breathes a sigh of relief and gazes down at the award in her hands. "I can't believe it. I didn't think it was real. I still don't fully believe it."

"You deserve it. That was a great speech. I'm proud of you."

She blushes at me. "I'm so glad you were there. I would have hated to face all of that alone."

"It's an honor to be your righthand man. I hope I can be there for all your big wins."

She squeezes my shoulder. "My righthand man. I like that."

I turn to smile up at her, and at that moment, like a bad smell, our good buddy Connor comes out from behind the nearest building to intercept us.

Mila groans. "What the hell do you want, Connor?"

He lowers his eyes to glare at me. "I told you to stay away from her. I told you to back off."

I snort at him and turn my chair away. I already see Andy coming toward us to intervene. "And look where that got you? Is that what you want—to wind up in the hospital again? Stay away from us, Connor."

I start to wheel my chair around him to continue to the limo, but he dives past me and tries to make a grab for Mila. Uh-huh. I don't think so.

I spin backward and chop my hand down across his wrist to knock his arm away. That one moment gives me enough time to pull my chair between him and her.

She rears away and steps behind me. I pivot around to confront him just as he straightens up to try again. "You better walk away right now," I snarl. "I won't give you another warning."

"You bastard!" he hisses. "I'll pay you back for this."

"You won't do anything about this. You're a jackass and a loser. Come near either of us again and I'll send you to the morgue next time. Be grateful I don't call the Police right now to arrest you for violating your restraining order. Now get the hell out of here and don't let me see your face again unless you want me to smash it in again even worse than the last time."

He glares at us, steals a glance at Andy coming up behind him, and Connor finally takes off into the city.

Mila lets out a gasp of relief. I turn around to face her. "Are you okay?" I ask.

She nods, but she's breathing too heavily to answer. Her eyes dart around everywhere.

I take her hand, but only for a minute. "Come on," I murmur. "Get in the car."

Chapter 19: Mila

A ndy waits for us in the penthouse parking garage while Giovanni and I get out of the limo. Andy shuts the door and all three of us get into the elevator together. We don't talk on our way upstairs.

We enter the upstairs corridor outside the penthouse before Andy breaks the silence. "Good night, Mr. Nowaczyk. Good night, Ms. Knapp. Call me if you need anything."

"Good night, Andy," Giovanni replies. "Thank you for your help tonight."

Andy goes off to one of the other doors and pulls out an electronic card to unlock it. That must be his apartment.

Giovanni lets me into his apartment and all the lights come on. I go to the living room and sit down on the couch to stare at the award in my hands. I haven't been able to stop staring at it all the way home.

The award ceremony stuns me much more than Connor confronting us or Giovanni threatening to send him to the morgue.

I can't believe I'm actually holding this award in my hands. It still doesn't seem real that the Infection Project could be this important—even though I know it is.

Giovanni has been acting so much more relaxed and happy since his photoshoot. I know the project affected all the subjects that way. I know because it affected me that way.

Seeing it happen to him up close and personal makes it mean something so much different. He's a completely new person. He's so much more settled in himself. He doesn't brood as much.

He drives himself just as hard if not harder, but he seems to have fallen into a groove with himself where he's okay with it all. He's okay with having to do things differently, work out differently, shower differently, and dress himself differently.

He no longer seems like he's going to war against the world every day just by getting out of bed. He seems to accept that who he is now is actually an improvement on what he was.

He switches off most of the lights in the kitchen and reduces the apartment to a soft, ambient glow. He wheels over to me, leans out of his chair, and moves himself over to sit next to me on the couch.

He locks eyes on me, takes the award out of my hands, and sets it on the coffee table so I pay attention to him instead.

"I want you to move in here with me, baby," he murmurs. "I don't want to spend a day or a night without you. I want you in my life always. I want us to face everything together."

I lower my eyes to our joined hands. I kind of always knew this was coming. I've been feeling it, too.

He doesn't wait for me to answer. He pulls me into his arms and down onto the couch. He has to sit up a second later to lift his legs onto the couch next to me, but he does it without thinking.

He doesn't try to apologize to me for the inconvenience. All those little details are normal to me now, too. I barely notice that he does things differently. It doesn't mean anything that I have to wait for him to straighten his legs before we can lie down together.

He pulls my head onto his chest and drapes his arm behind my shoulders. We both sink into this comfortable feeling.

"Thank you for protecting me tonight," I breathe into his shirt. "I'm really grateful that you were there. I've always worried that he would come after me if I told him no too many times."

He runs his fingers through my hair. "I would never let anything happen to you. I want Andy to start driving you around when you need to go anywhere. He can arrange to take each of us where we need to go and drive you while I'm at work."

I push myself up on my elbow to study him. "Don't you think you better talk to him about that? It will eat into his free time if he has to drive both of us. He could wind up working twice as much and have half as much free time as before. I'm sure your arrangement isn't as appealing to him this way as it was before."

"I already talked to him about it and he's fine with it. We came up with a new arrangement."

I frown at him. "You did? What is it?"

"He's divorced with three children. He and his ex share custody and he takes the kids to stay at his apartment every other week and half the school vacations."

My eyes fall out of their sockets. "I didn't know about that! You never told me."

He shrugs. "It was confidential. I didn't want to blab his personal business to someone he doesn't know. Anyway, his ex got sick a few months ago. She has terminal cancer and the doctors don't give her much more than a couple of months. His mother has been helping out with the kids when they go home to their mom. Andy is planning for his mother and the three kids to come live here with him full-time as soon as his ex dies. So it's a trade-off. He'll have less free time to do whatever he wants, but he won't be as on-call as he was before. You and I will have to work around his schedule the same way he'll have to work around ours. There may be times when we have to bring in a replacement driver if something in his personal life is more important and he has to put family first."

I blink at him. "That's incredible! When did all this happen?"

"Just this past week. I didn't want to say anything to you before we had a chance to talk about if you want to move in here with me or not." He pauses to let that sink in. *"Do* you want to move in here with me?"

I gulp. "I do....but...."

He raises his eyebrows. "But?"

I look away.

"Talk to me, baby," he murmurs. "Tell me what's on your mind. You say you want to but. So what's the but? I need to know."

I turn around and look at him. I realize the truth the instant I make eye contact with him.

The same thing happened that first night I spent with him. I wanted to, but doubts, fears, and insecurities got the better of me. I couldn't do it until he opened the door for me to step through it.

This is the same. I want to move in with him. I want to build a life with him and face everything together. I want that more than anything.

I need him to open the door for me—but he already has. He does it by sliding his hand up my back to my neck and steering my mouth into his kiss.

I can let it all go when I kiss him like this. I can feel how much my body wants to climb on top of him and feel him touching me, undressing me, possessing me, and making me his own.

I don't see his disability anymore—just like he doesn't see my flaws anymore. This is just the way we are. This is just the way we live. He does things his way and I do things my way.

His fingertips crawl down my thighs and he pulls my dress up—exactly the way he's been dreaming about doing since he first bought me this dress. I would have to be blind not to see the way he undresses me with his eyes.

His warm, muscular hands scoop around my ass and pull my thighs apart on top of him. He steers my hips into his hardness, buries my face between his legs, and lifts me to straddle his face.

We're already one. Me moving in here is inevitable. It may always have been inevitable since that first day we met at the library.

We get up off the couch afterward and I wait for him to get into his wheelchair so we can go upstairs to the bedroom—our bedroom—his and mine. I've already been living here for over a month. It's my room as much as his.

We get into bed together the same way we have these last few weeks. I get such a sense of love when I watch him hitch himself over to the bed, straighten his chair so he'll be able to get to it when he needs it, and go through all his little rituals to get ready for bed.

I trail my hand up and down his back while he sits there finishing a few things on his phone before he puts it away for the night. He still has a business to run. This is just the usual nighttime routine—nothing out of the ordinary.

He finally collapses back on the pillow, runs his fingers through his hair, and pulls me into his arms. "It's such a relief to know that you're here," he breathes. "I don't like to think about you being anywhere else."

I sink into his side and swallow a lump in my throat. "Thank you...for all of this."

He presses his nose and mouth into my hair and we both fall asleep like that. Feeling him next to me is the best medicine for a wounded soul. Everything is all right. I can rest here. I don't have to worry about anything else.

Chapter 20: Mila

I bend over to get something out of the fridge and take it over to the kitchen counter. The counters are all too low for me, so Giovanni has brought in a rolling kitchen island for me.

I have to bend over to stir things on the stove and get things out of the sink, but that all feels normal now, too. I'm living here. This is just the way we do things in our house.

"I want you to come by my office and see me today, baby," Giovanni tells me from his side of the counter. "If you aren't too busy."

I look up. "What for?"

"I want to talk to you about some projects we're doing. I want your input on them."

I frown at him. "But I don't have any expertise in your industry. I'm not in it."

"You're a photographer, so you have all the expertise you need. Besides, what I want your input on isn't industry related. It's artistic."

I frown at him. "I don't understand."

"I'll explain everything when you get there. What time will you be available?"

"Um...I have a meeting with a couple for another family photo-shoot. That's at ten and should take half an hour. Then I have a headshot photoshoot at eleven-thirty. Why don't we do it at one?"

He nods and picks up his coffee cup. "That will work."

He goes back to eating his breakfast, drinking his coffee, and noodling around on his phone before work. I don't know what this is all about, but I guess I'll find out when I get there.

Andy drives him to the Mammoth Media office building downtown and I kiss him goodbye in the back of the limo. Then Andy drives me to my old apartment. I have a studio here where I do headshots and other photoshoots that require a studio.

Giovanni and I have been talking about keeping the apartment just to function as my studio when I need one.

I don't know how I feel about that. I don't want to go back and forth, but setting up a new studio in one of his penthouse's spare rooms would be just as inconvenient to my clients as coming to my old apartment.

We haven't come to any conclusion yet, so I drop right back into my old routine of doing things the way I did before I met him. I finish the headshots and have my meeting with the couple that wants family photos.

I have to pull my head out of the clouds when Andy takes me back to the Mammoth building. This company really is mammoth. It's a force of nature in the advertising, entertainment, publish, and media world.

The building itself occupies a whole city block in midtown Manhattan. This place has everything from music studios, its own printing and publishing departments, whole sub-companies for advertising, and everything else in the media sector. Giovanni does it all.

I never thought I would live to see the day when I would set foot in this place. Everyone who works here is a trained industry professional. Some of these people even have multiple advanced degrees in their fields.

At least I'm not the only person in the building not wearing a business suit. Plenty of people wear casual and some of the recording engineers and professional musicians even wear grungy streetwear.

I also see plenty of models in skimpy outfits, photographers in hipster wear, and every other kind of person known to the human race.

I still feel out of place. I don't belong to this world and I never will. I may have just won the Annie Leibowitz Award for Excellence in Photography, but I'm still just a starving nobody doing headshots and family photoshoots to pay the bills.

I haven't made a penny off the Infection Project. I probably never will.

The project did get my name out there so more people come to me for all the other photography I do. That's about it—oh, and I met Giovanni through the project, too.

I walk through the massive lobby entrance. A big abstract sculpture hangs from the glass ceiling and reflects prismatic rainbows all over the lobby.

Voices throb through the building and people crisscross the floor, ride the elevators, and discuss everything they're working on.

I stop at the lobby reception desk. "I'm Mila Knapp," I tell the receptionist. "I have an appointment to see Giovanni Nowaczyk."

The receptionist smiles at me. "You can go right on in, Ms. Knapp. He's expecting you."

"Um...could you tell me where I'm supposed to go?"

"He's in his office on the fortieth floor." She points to the elevators. "Just go up there and you'll find him."

I get into the elevator and push the number forty button. A bunch of other people get on with me. They all push buttons for lower floors. I'm the only one going to the fortieth floor.

I'm the only one left in the elevator by the time the doors open for me to get out. I step out into a big, open-plan office with a bunch of standing workstations, couches, and sitting areas covering a wide shared space in the center.

Stately offices surround this open place. Massive windows give each office a sweeping panoramic view of New York in one direction or another.

Giovanni wheels out of a side office as soon as I step out of the elevator. "Ah! You're here! Excellent!" he exclaims. "Come on over here. I want you to take a look at something."

He turns his chair around and I follow him, but we get cut off by a middle-aged man coming out of a different office to one side.

He stops in his tracks and points at me. "Wait a minute. Mila Knapp, right?" He grabs my hand. "I'm a huge fan of your work."

"Um....thank you," I stammer.

"Mila, this is Mammoth Chief Operations Officer, Cal Wilber-force," Giovanni tells me.

"Um....hi." I shake Cal's hand.

"Are you interviewing to work here as a photographer?" he asks.

"No, she's here to have a meeting with me about the company's artistic direction," Giovanni cuts in. "Come in here, Mila. I want you to show you something."

I have to walk around Cal to follow Giovanni in the direction he was leading me to begin with. Cal takes a few steps to go with us, but he changes his mind before he gets there. Giovanni didn't invite him to join us.

The office behind us has been set up as a lounge or green room or something. It doesn't have any desks or computers or anything I would expect to find in an office.

It's just a good-sized living room with sectional couches arranged around a large coffee table. It's actually the perfect height for Giovanni to work at while he's sitting in his wheelchair.

He pulls up in front of a collection of glossy advertising images with text splashed across them. The ads are for Golden Road, a chain of malls across the country. The company is owned by Dante Helme.

"So what do you think?" Giovanni asks me.

"What do you mean?" I ask. "These look great."

"Don't give me that. Tell me what you really think."

I blink at him and then at the pictures. "That is what I really think. These are great. They're high-quality. They're vibrant. They capture the spirit of the campaign...."

He makes a face. "Is that all?"

"What else is there?"

"They aren't artistic."

"Sure, they are. I mean....look at them. They're very artistic." I frown at him. "Is this really what you brought me here for—to make them more artistic?"

"Of course! I told you I was trying to make our product more artistic—more like your work. Your work actually means something. It makes a statement. This doesn't."

"You don't want to make a statement and you don't want it to mean anything. You're advertising for a chain of malls. This isn't an art piece."

"It's both. There's no reason why we shouldn't make a statement and make it mean something, especially for an ad campaign. That's exactly how we would make the campaign memorable and the product stick in the customer's mind—if it meant something and made a statement."

"I'm not sure what to tell you. I mean....Mammoth is known for making a statement. Your work is known for being the highest quality and also very artistic."

"It isn't enough. It's too shallow and superficial. The level of artistic depth isn't where it should be."

"Are you sure? Your customers seem awfully satisfied."

"Well, I'm not. Take a look at these."

He scoops aside the Golden Road ad campaign and pulls out another stack of pictures. These are from a fashion spread with models posing for the camera.

"See what I mean?" he asks.

"Not really," I tell him. "I'm sorry. I'm not trying to be hard-headed. You cater to a certain dimension of the open market. That market expects a certain product from you and that's what you deliver. You're able to command a higher asking price than your competition because your work is so high-quality, so on-brand, and so relevant. I don't understand why you want to mess with a winning formula."

"I don't necessarily want to mess with it. I want to improve it." He waves at the fashion images. "Tell me how you would improve them."

I stare at them and then shrug. "I wouldn't. I would leave them the way they are."

"Come on!" he urges. "Help me out. I want to take this company in a new artistic direction. I want our work to have depth—which it doesn't now."

"But the market isn't asking for depth."

"Of course it is! Don't you remember the 'Just Do it' Nike campaign or the 'We Can Do It' ad campaign from World War 2? We could be doing stuff like that. We could be doing campaigns that change the world and have an impact on the whole culture." He turns to me. "I want you to become our new artistic director. I know our work is high quality, but we can do better than just catering to what the customer wants. We can give the customers what they want, but we can also give society what it wants—which is impact. I want you to lead the company to the next level of artistic style, aesthetic, and depth."

I frown at him. "I don't think what I do is compatible with what you're talking about. I don't think they're even in the same universe."

"That's exactly what I need you for. I want you to mold, steer, and inspire the company's future artistic vision."

I open my mouth and look down at the pictures in front of me. They really are perfect—flawless, even. That's the problem. They're flawless.

Like magic, he takes out the Golden Road pictures and lays them in front of me so I can see them all side by side.

These pictures are perfect for what they are. They're ads for a business and fashion spreads for a magazine. That's all they are. They don't cross over into artistic photography. That isn't what they're trying to d o.

I get a flashback of some of the speakers' comments at the awards ceremony. Annie Leibowitz started working as a photographer for Rolling Stone Magazine. That's how she first made her first statement pieces—from inside the industry.

Giovanni is right that these pictures don't have depth. They aren't artistic in their tone. They aren't trying to be. That's the problem.

Mammoth is already an icon of aesthetics and artistic style, but it could be legendary if it upped its game and made every campaign, every spread, and every single photograph as iconic as that.

That's what makes the Infection Project work. Every single photograph tells a story, makes a statement, and means something.

Could I really do that? I've always considered my work antagonistic to the corporate world.

I could have gotten a job at Mammoth a long time before I ever met Giovanni. He just never would have found out about me. We never would have had anything to do with each other.

I look up into his eyes. He stares back at me all overflowing with hopeful anticipation. He believes in this mission. He really wants to take Mammoth there. He just doesn't know how.

"All right," I tell him. "I'll do it."

Chapter 21: Giovanni

I wheel my chair up to the boardroom table and park in the empty place at the far end. The rest of the executive and artistic teams assemble around the room. Cal comes over to me. "Do you need me to help you set anything up?"

"I don't need anything," I reply. "I'm not conducting this meeting."

He frowns at me. "You aren't?"

"Nope. I'm only here as an impartial observer."

He's still frowning at me when Mila walks in. She wears one of her casual outfits, but she still looks stunning. She doesn't look out of place at all even though everyone else in the room wears a suit. Even the women wear suits.

Cal jolts out of his skin when he sees her, but it's time for me to call this meeting to order. "Let's all take our seats," I tell everyone. "I want you all to meet Mammoth's new artistic director, Mila Knapp."

A bunch of people gasp and stare at her. Mila plays it off and strides to the front of the room where she stands at the other end of the table. She acts so calm about all of this.

She opens her laptop, hooks it up to the room's media system, and opens a slideshow on the screen behind her head.

"This is a series of photography shots that have caused seismic cultural shifts in Western society over the last hundred years," she tells everyone. "I'm sure each of you has seen these images dozens or maybe even hundreds of times."

Sanders Faulkner, our Director of Fashion Photography, turns to me. "Um....why are we looking at this?"

"You're looking at it because each of these images had a cultural impact that touched millions or even billions of people," Mila interrupted. "You're looking at it because each of these images touched far more people than their original target audience. Take the Marlboro Man, for example."

She brings up images of the iconic Marlboro Man carrying his saddle, leaning on a fence with his cigarette hanging out of his mouth, and his hat shading his eyes.

"These images imprinted on an entire generation what manhood was supposed to be," she goes on. "This archetype spread far beyond cigarette smokers and influenced the entire culture. This image from the war in Afghanistan imprinted on an entire generation the ravages of war." She flicks through a dozen other pictures and finally settles on some of Annie Leibowitz's most iconic portraits. "Mammoth could be having that kind of impact. You're focusing on your target market—and that's what you should be doing—but you could be doing more. You could be touching the lives of people far beyond your current campaign. You could be influencing the whole society—not just your client's target audience."

"How are we supposed to do that?" Cal asks.

Sanders raises both hands. "Excuse me, Ms. Knapp. I understand your show is considered the hottest thing right now, but what you do isn't even in the same category as what we do."

"Maybe that's the problem," Mila told him. "Maybe the problem is that you don't see your work as artistic at all. You're insulting your audience's intelligence by assuming they don't want something more meaningful with more depth—something that speaks to their desire for more—something that speaks to their desire to mold the future. If you don't mold it, someone else will. If you don't get inside their heads and start taking up residence there, someone else will. Your products and your clients' products could be so much more memorable instead of just another trinket the customer can buy. They already have enough of that."

Sanders turns back to me. "Why are we even listening to this? Why are we taking the opinion of an amateur who has no industry experience at all?"

"You're an industry professional and maybe even an industry leader, Mr. Faulkner," Mila tells him. "And yet you're the one who's overseeing the production of all this trivial, superficial, throwaway ad copy. You're producing tons and tons of work year after year that no one is ever going to remember."

Sanders doesn't even look at her. He continues to face me. "Aren't you even going to say anything about this?"

"Why do you think I'm here, Mr. Faulkner?" Mila asks him. "Do you honestly think I don't have anything better to do than tell you how you can improve your work? I didn't just stroll in off the street to come in here to insult you. Giovanni invited me here. He's the one who asked me to come on board as your new artistic director. This wasn't my idea at all."

Sanders spins around to stare at her. "You're lying!"

"Don't you think he would have said something by now to tell me to leave the building if I was really just some amateur off the street?"

Sanders whips around to confront me. "Is that true?"

"She's right, Sanders," I tell him. "Your work is totally forgettable. All of it is. Each of you is responsible for overseeing whole departments that produce entirely forgettable work. You all encourage your staff and subordinates to make this work as forgettable, as boring, and as mediocre as possible."

Our graphic design director, Betty Calhoun, gasps across the table. "We do not! Our customers are thrilled with our work! They can't get enough of it! They're the ones who say it's iconic."

"It could be a lot better—and it's going to be. That's where this company is heading." I point to the front of the room. "Go on with your presentation, Mila."

She goes on with her presentation, shows a few more examples, and then shows examples from our recent campaigns. She holds them up side by side.

Our work really is meaningless compared to these iconic images. She talks at length about what she wants each department to do and how she wants them to think about ways to change it.

The execs, directors, and department heads slink out of the room with their tails between their legs as soon as she finishes the meeting.

"They didn't take it very well, did they?" she murmurs.

"They'll get used to it. Today is only the first day. They'll come around and get on board."

"And if they don't?"

I shrug. "Then they'll get left behind. I don't want to wait anymore. We have things to do. Don't let anyone tell you to change what you're doing. Just keep pushing through."

"I hope you're right."

She leaves and I go to my office. I check a few different proofs of magazines coming out this week and the covers for some of our nonfiction books.

I leave my office two hours later and go downstairs to the photography department. Sanders was overseeing a shoot there today and I know Mila was planning to sit in on it.

I get there just in time to see her standing off to one side. Sanders goes from one model to the other putting them into different poses and straightening their hair and outfits.

Mila steps out of line and cuts him off. "No, no, no, no, no," she interrupts. "This is all wrong."

He spins around to glare at her. "You shouldn't be down here. Please leave."

"Actually, Mr. Faulkner, if you check the contract I just signed with Mammoth Media, my new position gives me open access to all departments and creative decision-making power over anything that could directly impact the company's public profile—and I think this shoot qualifies. Now pay attention and you just might learn something. If I can do it, you can do it, too."

She approaches the models and repositions them. She puts all their arms down and in some cases places the models' hands on their hips. Then Mila removes most of the frills, hats, and accessories surrounding the models' heads.

"What are you doing?!" Sanders practically shrieks. "Do you know how long we've been working to get these outfits right?!"

"You aren't doing a very good job, are you?" Mila counters. "This photoshoot is for a makeup line. These outfits are distracting the viewer from seeing the models' faces—which is exactly what you want the viewer to see. You even put a fan in front of this model's face to block her from the camera. What is it that you don't want the viewer to see, Mr. Faulkner? That's what your viewer will be asking themselves if you can't even show the makeup you're supposed to be advertising."

Sanders gasps in scandalized horror. I stay in the background where neither he nor Mila will see me. I don't want to intervene. He and everyone else in my company is going to have to get on board with this new direction.

Mila goes through the models one after another and eventually changes all their outfits to neutrals. Then she moves the photographers way closer to the models so the cameras focus right on their faces.

"Reduce the saturation," she tells one of the photographers. "And wash out the color palette."

"You can't do that!" Sanders storms. "You'll ruin the whole shoot!"

She gives him a look of withering disdain and points at the photographer. "Do it—and all of you models stop smiling. Keep your expressions neutral but keep your eyes bright. Look right up into the light."

The photographers start snapping pictures. Mila stands off to one side instructing the models to turn one way or the other, rearrange their order, raise or lower their heads, or to part or close their lips.

She also gives instructions to the photographers on what shots to take, how to take them, and from which angles.

I stick around a little longer. Sanders paces in the back of the room shaking his head and fuming. I can already see where this is going.

I go upstairs to my office, get on my computer, and pull up the proofs from his previous shoots for this same campaign. She's right. The models stand in totally contrived poses like they're trying to make themselves as ridiculous as possible.

Sanders has dressed them in garish, blinding, extravagant outfits no sane person would ever wear in public—or probably even in private.

The outfits, the poses, and the overall aesthetics stop the viewer from even looking at the models' makeup. I wouldn't know the ad was for makeup.

Sanders shows up right on time half an hour after the shoot wraps. "What the hell were you thinking bringing that troll on board this company, Giovanni?!" he rages.

I lean back in my chair like I wasn't expecting him to come and confront me like this. "Troll? She isn't a troll, Sanders. She's an extremely talented photographer. I don't think you have ever won the Annie Leibowitz Award for Excellence in Photography, have you?"

"She isn't Annie Leibowitz!" he thunders. "She's a nobody!"

"She isn't a nobody and she did win the award—so I think she knows something about photography that you don't. You either play ball and take her recommendations or you find another job."

His jaw drops, and right then, I get a notification on my computer. The photographers from the makeup shoot have just logged their proofs onto the system for everyone in upper management to see.

I open the folder. Sanders doesn't ask for permission to come around my desk and see them.

The pictures spray across the screen and I look through them one face after another. The closeups, the neutral outfits, the washed-out color palette, and the reduced saturation strip the pictures of every extraneous detail.

They leave nothing but the models and their bare makeup. I can even see the glossy sheen of their lipstick.

Their neutral expressions make each woman look timeless, classic, and....well, iconic. They could be any woman and every woman.

Their expressions and the angles of their heads turn each picture into a portrait for the ages. These women paint a picture of what every woman wants to look like.

The close-up shots even show some of the models' imperfections through their makeup, but like all of Mila's work, these imperfections only make the women look more human and relatable.

Sanders and I stare at the images in stunned silence. I don't know what to say except that she did it. She made her point and then some.

Sanders stands up, stares at the screen for another long, meaningful silence, and walks out of the office without another word. Maybe now he'll realize that he can do it and he has to do it.

Chapter 22: Mila

I walk into Giovanni's penthouse apartment, flop on the couch, and sprawl there with an agonized groan. I throw my arm over my face to block out the world.

I'm home sooner than Giovanni. He got tied up at the office. I don't know when he'll get home.

I should get up and make dinner, but Giovanni rolls in right behind me.

"Hey! Where did you come from?" I ask. "How did you get here so fast?"

"Um..." He looks around. "Andy drove me. How else do you think I got here?"

"I didn't think I left the office that long ago. Andy just dropped me off and went back for you. I thought you would stay at the office much longer."

He frowns at me. "Are you feeling okay? Why are you lying there on the couch?"

"I'll get up soon. I just want to lie here feeling sorry for myself for a little while longer. Now I remember why I never went into corporate photography. I didn't want to deal with all the personalities."

He chuckles while he puts his laptop bag on the kitchen counter and starts taking off his jacket. "You really shattered Sanders's world, didn't you?"

I groan again and wind up sitting up. "Did you see the outfits he put on those models? I mean, Jesus! What exactly does he think he's advertising?"

He laughs. "You didn't see the proofs from his previous shoots. They were much worse."

I narrow my eyes at him. "You don't think I made the wrong call, do you? I mean....he is the Director of Fashion Photography."

He won't stop smiling. He rolls his wheelchair toward me and holds out his phone so I can see the screen.

I flip through the proofs from today's shoot. They look outstanding. They look as iconic and universal as I hoped they would.

"You have nothing to worry about," he tells me. "Just keep doing what you're doing."

"I won't be able to turn everything into a black and white. I've already done that once."

"You don't have to turn it into a black and white to make it timeless and meaningful. I want you to work on the Golden Road campaign next."

"What's wrong with what you have?"

"I just think we can do better. We won't scrap the old material. Just see what you can do with it. We can always fall back on the old material if you can't come up with anything better."

"What kind of vibe were you going for with that—that you didn't capture with the first attempt?"

He shrugs. "The name is Golden Road—so I was thinking something exquisite, exotic, and luxury."

"I was thinking the same thing."

He beams at me. "Would you like to go out to dinner tonight to celebrate?"

"Naw. I'll cook you something." I go into the kitchen and start rummaging around in the fridge. "We need to do some shopping and bring in groceries. We're running low."

"I'll send you the link for the online delivery service I use. You can order from them and they'll send everything over."

I take a bunch of ingredients out of the pantry and heat up a frying pan on the stove. "Was there a specific time you wanted to work on the Golden Road campaign tomorrow? I have an optometrist appointment at eleven, so we'll have to work around that."

"I have meetings all morning, so why don't we meet up at one? We can go over it then."

I nod and get busy cutting up the vegetables. Then I set the table while Giovanni does his workout. He comes in all showered and changed just as I'm serving the food. He wears a pair of casual black pants and a bright red Polo shirt.

He pulls up his chair at the table and I sit down opposite him. "Thank you for this," he tells me. "I feel like I should reciprocate."

"I don't mind. I like cooking for you."

"I bet you don't like bending over that stove, though, do you? Maybe we should get some alternate arrangement for you."

"No, no! Just leave it the way it is. It isn't that big a deal."

"I don't mind. This apartment wasn't designed for a person to stand in the kitchen."

"I wonder why not if the previous owner was able to use weight machines for his legs."

He shrugs. "We'll probably never know."

"The kitchen is fine the way it is. Just leave it alone. I don't mind it."

He gazes at me across the table. The sparkle in his eyes could mean any of a dozen things.

"What?" I ask.

"You were mind-blowing today. You exceeded all my expectations."

I look down at my plate. "I didn't do anything except piss a lot of people off."

"You accomplished what I brought you in to accomplish. You gave that shoot the depth and gravitas it needed. It never would have gotten that from Sanders. That's what I need you for. None of them sees it."

I don't know what to say, so I change the subject to the other projects he wants me to completely derail.

He talks a lot about what he wants and where he sees the company going. He wants to change literally every project on his books—some of which the clients have already approved.

"Dante will be cool with whatever we decide to do," he tells me. "He'll be right on board with it if he thinks we're trying to make it better."

"Have you talked to him about the Golden Road project?"

"Not since I decided to bring you on. We can talk to him about it at the gala."

"But didn't you say the gala was for socializing? He probably won't want to talk business then."

He snorts. "The vast majority of conversation at the gala is business. That's what passes for socializing in the club."

"Really? Doesn't that get kinda boring after a while?"

He laughs. "That's why we hang out together. We're the only people who understand that socializing is business and business is socializing. All of us consider talking business the most enjoyable form of socializing. That's why we socialize with each other—because we understand each other."

I try to shrug it off. "I don't think I'll ever understand that."

He takes my hand across the table. "I don't want you to. I don't want you to be one of them. I value you for other things—like your tits."

I laugh and pull away from him to clear the table. He does something on his laptop until it's time for us to go upstairs.

He comes up behind me while I'm taking my clothes off. He has to park his wheelchair sideways so he doesn't bump into me.

He starts by raking his fingernails up the outsides of my thighs, circling my waist, and rocking my hips back. He buries his face between my thighs from behind, inhales deeply, and roots around to push my legs apart.

I gasp and catch my breath. He turns me on more than I can stand. My flesh throbs between my legs, and like magic, he runs his hand up between my thighs and rubs me through my pants.

I rock on that hand and moan as the dizzy waves of pleasure sweep over me. I fall forward and support myself on my elbows on the dresser to ride my hips back toward him.

He grabs my pants and pulls them down to bare my ass right in his face. He burrows between my legs from behind and his hot tongue lights me on fire. I sob in agony as his fingers delve deep into my saturated tissues. I need him so bad.

He sees exactly what I need, grabs my shirt, and strips it and my bra down so he can paw my breasts from behind. I want him to stand up and nail me right here against the dresser, but that will never happen.

I shut my eyes, throw back my head, and imagine that he's doing it right now. He's bumping my ass hard against the dresser. These aren't his fingers inside me.

He pulls out and steers my hips back to sit on his lap facing away from him. I didn't see when or how he got his fly open, but he lowers me down right on top of his throbbing, straining meat.

I scream as my weight drives him to my deepest, innermost depths. He rests his hand on the back of my neck, tips me forward, and pulls me back into a delirious, rocking beat.

I support myself against the dresser and let my spine arch the way he wants it to. I want him to see me exposed and desperate for him. I want him to see me letting go of all inhibitions and giving everything I have to our time together.

He doesn't let me stop until I wind myself up to a screaming orgasm. He keeps grabbing my breasts in hard pinches, slipping his hand between my thighs from the front to rub me into a frenzy, and tightening his grip on the back of my neck in a firm commanding hold.

I can't get enough when he treats me like this. I love that he owns me and conquers me. I want him to do more of it, but he always holds back to avoid hurting or scaring me.

He waits until I completely collapse in sobbing ecstasy. He lets go of me and pulls his wheelchair away with me still sitting on his lap.

He steers me toward the bed before I know what hit me. He parks there while I get off, strips off his clothes, and climbs onto the bed with me.

I take the rest of my clothes off and curl up on my side still trembling with pleasure while he gets undressed and moves his wheelchair around to its usual place.

He needs to be able to get into it quickly and easily if he needs to go to the bathroom or to get up for some other reason.

I'm starting to drift off when he stretches out next to me. I barely open my eyes to kiss him back. I crawl into his arms and press my body against him.

He stiffens at that touch and clamps his hand on my ass in a tight squeeze. He lets his fingers trail a little lower toward that cleft of wetness he just created for himself.

His touch electrifies me, and before I can even move, he pulls away and pushes me down on my stomach on the bed.

He rolls on top of me from behind, pins me down, and husks in my ear. I've never heard that deep, primal growl from him before. "I want you," he snarls.

I yelp when I feel his hard spike stabbing between my legs from behind. I stiffen, but he clamps his arms around me, and in one swift motion, he locks his other hand around my throat. "You're mine," he hisses. "Did you think you could get away from me?"

My every nerve sizzles with danger—and then that sensation turns to pure ravenous excitement. I want him to. I want him to take me that way. I want him to get rough.

He lets go immediately, rolls off me, and relaxes on his back staring at the ceiling. My eyes drift open. He's still awake.

"What's wrong?" I ask.

"Nothing." He kisses me on the side of the cheek. "I love you. You're tired. You should go to sleep."

"Are you....?" I hesitate. Is he going to just forget what he just did? Does he really expect me to just forget it?

He glances over at me. "Don't worry. Everything's all right."

I gulp. "Have you ever done that to a girl before?"

"Done what?"

"What you just did to me—putting your hand on my throat and making it out that you were going to take me that way?"

He looks away. "Yes, I have, but I don't want to do it to you."

"Why not?"

"I already told you. I don't want to treat you the way I treated them. I respect you too much."

"But.....I want you to. I want you to get rough with me."

"No, you don't," he mumbles. "Not like that."

"Don't you think I know what I like and what I want? Do you think I would say it if I didn't want you to?"

"You didn't ask what else I did with them."

"Maybe I want you to do that to me, too. Did you ever think of that? We could be like that. I want you to."

He gulps visibly. He won't look at me. "I don't trust myself."

I can't stand it when he acts like this. I want him to be strong and confident.

I sit up, grab my pants, fish my phone out of my pocket, and navigate to the pictures I took of him by the pool. I turn the phone around to show him the picture. "What would he do?"

He stares at the picture for a second and shoots off the bed much faster this time. He rolls me onto my back, pins my wrists to the mattress, and kisses me ravenously for a second before he flips me onto my stomach again.

He snarls in my ear in wordless madness, clamps his hand around my throat, and drives his other hand between my legs.

I gasp out as his fingers find me—and then he drills into me from behind. His powerful arms clamp me in a death grip. That tight hold sets off a similar reaction in me and I start to struggle. I don't want to get away. I want him to do it like this.

The energy between us makes me do it. It happens on pure instinct and he responds by crushing me in a death grip. My struggling only triggers him to strike harder. He slams me down on the mattress hammering me into another screaming orgasm.

He doesn't stop—not then, not ever. The minute he sends me reeling into the stratosphere, he lets go of me, pushes himself up on his arms, and pounds me from behind even harder.

I claw at the mattress trying in every possible way to contain all this energy pulsing through me. I can't cope with it. I've never felt anything like this in my life.

I crawl up to the headboard trying to hold onto something solid—something to anchor myself. I want to get up on my knees, but I can't—not without leaving him behind. He wouldn't be able to do it to me there.

He plants his hand on my back right at the base of my neck, holds me down, and doesn't let me go anywhere else while he drills me to the stars.

He finally lowers himself on top of me again, takes one fistful of my hair, and pries my head back to cram his hot, scorching mouth against my ear. "Mine!" he snarls. "Mine!"

I explode into another spinning tornado of rapture at that word. I'm his. I'll never escape, thank goodness. I'll stay with him in this halo of love forever. I don't want to go anywhere or be anywhere else.

Chapter 23: Mila

I rest my hand on Giovanni's shoulder when we walk into the grand ballroom of the Four Seasons Hotel. This is the first Billionaires' Club gala I've attended.

"I don't see any of the cannibals' victims turning on the spit over an open flame," I remark when I see all the fancy people dressed up in tuxes and evening gowns.

He laughs. "That's because you just showed up. They'll put you on the spit as soon as you walk in."

I shot him a smirk and he grins at me. "Just tell them to put me out of my misery first."

"Where's the fun in that? We want to watch you writhe in torment."

I have to steady my nerves before I walk in there. Everyone here is dressed to the hilt. The women all wear expensive gowns and most are dripping with jewelry. They glide around the ballroom on the arms of some of the richest men in New York.

Giovanni rolls right in like he belongs here. He does belong here. He's a member of the club and I'm his date. I hope no one here thinks I'm one of his hired girls as he calls them. I can just imagine what people here think of me.

Dante Helme comes up to us first and shakes Giovanni's hand. "Hey! You made it. And who is this ravishing creature? It can't be Mila Knapp. I don't believe it. You lucky son of a bitch!"

Dante takes my hand and makes me blush. "It's an honor to meet you, Mr. Helme."

"You better not start calling me that. Where have you been hiding her, Giovanni? You didn't tell me you were seeing anyone."

"I wanted to keep her to myself. This is the first club event we've been able to come to since we started going out. Oh, by the way, Dante. Mila is helping out Mammoth with the Golden Road campaign."

Dante's eyes fly open. "Really? That's fantastic! How much is he paying you? I promise it isn't enough."

I turn bright red. "We'll see how it turns out. You might really hate it."

"I doubt it. I absolutely love your work."

Giovanni nudges me and jerks his head at Dante. Dante notices and glances back and forth between us. "What's wrong? Is something wrong with the campaign? Just tell me now if it is."

"Nothing is wrong with it," I tell him. "It's just....."

Giovanni takes my phone out of his jacket pocket and hands it to me. I open it and show Dante a bunch of pictures in my gallery.

His jaw drops when he sees what I've been doing with his campaign. "We still have the old proofs in case you don't like it," I tell him. "We can fall back on Giovanni's original concept—whichever one you like better. This is just experimental, you understand."

"This is brilliant!" Dante murmurs. "This is.....it's.....it's genius."

"It's all hers," Giovanni interjects. "You don't think I could come up with something like this, do you?"

Dante gulps, hands my phone back, and stares at me with a very different expression on his face. "This is incredible. I love it."

"Oh, phew!" I pass my hand across my brow and give my phone back to Giovanni for safekeeping. "I was so worried about showing it to you. I thought it would ruin the whole evening."

"No! No, it's perfect. I never thought...." He looks down at Giovanni.

"You can say it," Giovanni tells him. "You never thought I could come up with this and I couldn't. That's why I brought Mila on board. She's going to retool our company and make it a thousand times better than it was."

"Wow," Dante exclaims. "Color me flabbergasted."

Neither of us can say anything else before a bunch of other people gather around all talking at once. They all greet Giovanni. The men shake hands with him and some even bend all the way over to hug him.

The women kiss him on the cheek and he kisses some of their hands. None of them will stop smiling.

Just as many people make an enormous fuss over me. These are the most powerful, most influential billionaires in the country and they treat *me* like a celebrity.

They all want to shake my hand. Some even ask for my autograph or ask if they can take selfies with me. I go along with it. My head starts spinning. I can't even remember half their names or who they're connected with.

They all want to talk about the Infection Project. Some even want to invest in it even though it isn't a moneymaking venture. Others just want to talk about people they know or close personal relatives who have had their lives changed by the project.

Others want to talk about the Annie Leibowitz Award and all the other stuff I'm working on. Then the shit hits the fan when Dante chimes in and tells them about me working for Mammoth. He tells me to show them all the pictures he showed me.

All the rest of the billionaires start bombarding me and Giovanni with questions about how the rest of the club members can get me to work on their marketing material, too.

I keep my left hand on his shoulder the whole time. I don't want to get lost in the mayhem. I hear him talking to dozens of people. I'm too distracted by my own conversations. I can't hear a word he says.

The commotion eventually dies down and everyone remembers to talk to each other as well as us. We've barely made it more than a dozen feet inside the ballroom.

Things quiet down after that. Giovanni takes me around and introduces me to everyone one couple at a time. I can remember their names and make the connections between them now.

First he introduces me to Kevin Drake, the club's membership officer. He, Dante, Judah Hayes, Jackson Metcalfe, Rory Kahn, and Lane Prince are the current officers.

The billionaires and their wives are all super nice. The longer I spend in this room, the easier it becomes to tell who is actually in a relationship with one of the guys.

I definitely start to pick out a few escorts and random girls the younger, single guys brought along as dates. The escorts and single girls wear a lot more jewelry and go to much greater lengths to compete against each other and every other woman in the room.

The billionaires' wives keep to themselves and don't mix with these girls—or maybe it's the girls who don't mix with the billionaires' wives. The billionaires' wives are too busy talking to each other even to notice the single girls.

The billionaires' wives all seem to have a lot to say to each other. They talk away like old friends, catch up on each other's lives and families, and I even catch some of them asking Vivian Salazar about renovations to her house.

The women also talk business. Piper Legrange is representing Niko Holloway in a civil suit for breach of contract against some construction contractor.

I can't be sure, but it sounds like Samantha Mulholland and Melody Gottlieb are in business together doing something or other.

I'm just starting to get a powerful feeling that I really don't belong here when a much younger woman comes up to me and takes my hand. She can't be much older than I am. She may even be younger.

"Hi there," she greets me. "I'm Emberlynn Rhinehart. I'm Dante's wife."

My jaw hits the floor. "You're....his wife?"

She laughs at my reaction. "We have kind of an age difference."

"Kind of! Holy crap!"

She won't stop blushing. "I know. He just told me you're working on his ad campaign now. He's super excited about it."

I look away. "I'm glad someone is."

"Aren't you? He said the pictures you showed him were stunning."

"I'm just getting used to this whole corporate thing. I've worked so hard to stay out of it."

"I know what you mean. I did the same thing—and then I decided it wasn't for me and I bailed."

"Really? Why?"

"Dante and I adopted two little boys. Things just got too busy at home. I mean....I didn't quit the company entirely. I just took a massive step back and let someone else take over running everything. Now I'm more of just a figurehead they bring out when they want to solicit investment."

"What's your business?" I ask.

"I founded the MegaDome Experience."

My mouth falls open a second time. "No, you didn't."

She blushes even more. "Don't tell anyone."

"But that's....like....that's huge! Are you kidding me? Holy crap!" My hand flies to my head. "I don't believe it."

"Giovanni was one of my start-up investors. The concert wouldn't have gotten off the ground without him."

Giovanni comes rolling over to us just then. "Hello, you two. I hope you're behaving yourselves."

"I was just telling Mila about your checkered past as a MegaDome investor," Emberlynn tells him.

"I still am one. Thank you, by the way. I still think you should have sold it to me."

"Of course you do. You would be the world's wealthiest man now if I had."

He smiles at her and slips his hand into mine. "Are you doing okay?"

"Yeah." I turn to one of the passing waiters and grab a glass of champagne. "I need a drink."

They both laugh. "I'm going over there to talk to Kevin about doing a campaign for him," Giovanni tells me. "He wants to talk to you about it, too, but let me warm him up first, okay?"

"Okay. You know where I am if you want to find me."

He motors off into the crowd. Emberlynn lays her hand on my arm as soon as he gets out of earshot. "You are so good for him!" she murmurs.

I blush, and right then, Dante comes over to us. "I have never seen Giovanni so happy, Mila. You are exactly what he needs."

"I was just telling her the same thing," Emberlynn adds. "This is the first time he's ever gotten serious about anyone."

"It obviously suits him," Dante goes on. "He looks like he's on the moon."

I glance over at Giovanni. His friends are just welcoming him into a circle of men across the room. They all clap him on the shoulders and smile at him. He beams back at them.

Is he telling them how happy he is with me? I don't even have to ask. I see him smiling at me that way all the time. I know I make him happy—as happy as he makes me.

I get swept back into conversation with the other billionaires' wives. I'm the only woman here who is in a serious relationship with one of them who isn't already married. Some of them even have kids at home.

The women talk business as much as anything else—and they all want to talk to me about Mammoth's new direction. The billionaires all use Mammoth for their marketing media, so whatever Mammoth is doing *is* their business.

Just as many people want to talk to me about the Infection Project, what I do for a living, and how it all works. They're all amazed when I tell them how Giovanni and I met at the library.

"It sounds like fate," Piper remarks.

"It certainly does," Samantha agrees.

"Do you think you'll stay on at Mammoth?" Emberlynn asks. "Do you think you'll move into the corporate world?"

"I really don't know what's going to happen," I reply. "This is all so new to me. Working at Mammoth is really still in the experimental phases—and the other directors and department heads might start erecting the guillotine if I make them change too much."

The other women laugh. I only partly mean it as a joke. I don't know what the future holds.

My life is already turning into something I barely recognize. Where will it turn next? I couldn't predict it even if I wanted to.

Chapter 24: Giovanni

Mila slips her arms around me in my office and kisses me. "Play nice with the other children, okay?" she tells me.

"No, I won't," I counter. "I'm going to go out there and beat the shit out of little Tommy Johnson just as soon as you leave."

She laughs and stands up. "Give the kid a break. He has a rough home life."

"How is that my problem?"

She turns away, opens her purse, and sticks her phone in it. "I'll be back from my optometrist appointment no later than twelve. Then we can meet to talk about the Golden Road campaign and decide what we're going to do about it."

"Don't we already know what we're going to do about it? Dante loved what you showed him at the gala. I thought you were ready to go with that."

"Do *you* love it? Is this what *you* want?"

"It's more of what I want than it was."

"Do you want to make any changes to it or try another concept?"

"I don't think we should be shooting for perfection at this point. I think we should just aim for improvement and a more real expression of our vision as a company—which this concept is. I think we should go for it."

"Then let's just meet to discuss the finer design elements like fonts and copy placement and that kind of thing."

I nod. She kisses me again. "Bye."

"See you later. Have a good appointment."

She leaves. I go off to put out another flame war between the photography department and the graphics design department. None of them wants to accept that we're changing the design they worked so hard to create.

I let my head fall on my arms after the great confrontation. The departments' jobs are to execute the concept the creative team sets out for them to execute.

If we decide it isn't good enough and needs to change, then the department's job is to change it, not to argue with me about it.

I drag my head up and get through a few more executive meetings that don't have anything to do with the company's artistic direction, thank Almighty God. I'm getting really sick and tired of pulling teeth on this one.

Mammoth didn't get to be as big and successful as it is without my artistic vision. If I don't think it's going in the right direction, then it isn't. I don't see anyone else around here coming up with any artistic visions—except Mila, of course.

I check the time on my phone. It's a quarter after twelve. That's strange. I wonder why she hasn't come back yet. I send her a text. *Did you run away with the optometrist?*

I get another phone call just then and I don't think about Mila or my meeting with her until five minutes to one. I check my phone. She hasn't even read my text yet. Now I know something is wrong.

I cross the fortieth floor to the lounge room where we agreed to talk about the Golden Road campaign. I would pace around waiting for her to show up, but pacing doesn't really work the same way when you're in wheelchair.

I lock my brakes and take out my phone to do a few other tasks while I wait. Maybe she just got held up. She doesn't come.

I navigate to Andy's number to see if he picked her up at the right time. Then I remember that he didn't drive her to the appointment. The optometrist's office is right around the corner from the Mammoth building. She walked to the appointment and she planned to walk back.

I wait until quarter after one. She doesn't come. She still hasn't read my text.

I leave the building without telling anyone where I'm going, burn rubber around the corner, and wheel up to the optometrist's reception desk.

"Hi!" the chirpy teenage receptionist greets me. "Do you have an appointment?"

"I'm not here for an appointment. I'm looking for Mila Knapp. She had an appointment earlier and now she's missing. Could you tell me if she left the appointment at the right time?"

The girl checks the computer. "Um...yes, Sir. She left at eleven-thirty."

I frown to myself. That's an hour and a half ago. Mila shouldn't have taken that long to walk back to the office.

I check my phone again. Is she ignoring my texts? Did something happen that made her think she wanted to end it with me? Is this her way of walking out of my life forever?

I can't stand this. I call Andy to come and drive me to her old apartment building, but of course I can't get in. I run into the same problem when I face the steps to the front door.

I call her. The phone rings and rings and rings. It doesn't even switch to voice mail. Something is definitely wrong. Andy stands off to one side watching in silence. No one has to explain the situation to me.

I hang up and make another phone call to Jackson Metcalfe. "What's up, buddy?" he answers.

"I need a favor, Jackson," I tell him. "A big favor."

"Name it, pal. I'm your man."

I give him a quick rundown of the problem. "I'm on my way over right now," he tells me. "Stay where you are."

He practically teleports to my location and shows up in his big black Range Rover. He never drives a limo. He's a car guy. He likes driving a real car.

He squints up at the building. "Do you know which apartment she's in?" he asks.

"No, I've obviously never set foot in the building."

He smirks at me. "Of course not. Stay here....I mean....you know what I mean."

He walks into the building. The door is unlocked at this time of day. God only knows what he's doing in there, but if Jackson can't get it done, it can't be done. If you want something done, he's the man to call.

He stays in the building for a long time—way too long. My nerves are nearing the breaking point when he comes out an hour later.

"What's going on?" I ask. "Is she in there?"

"Yeah." He winces. "She's in there."

"What's the problem? She won't answer my calls or my texts."

"She won't tell me what the problem is. She won't talk to me, either. I can't tell you anything except that she's extremely upset and she wants you to leave. She wants everyone to leave her alone."

"Why?" I hear my voice shaking. "Can't you at least tell me why?"

His cheek spasms when he looks down at me. "I wish I could, but she wouldn't tell me why. She just said to leave her alone. She's.....I don't know if I should tell you this, but she was crying too hard to say anything else."

I look away. It's over between us. That's what this is.

Jackson crushes my shoulder in a death grip. "Go home, man. You can't do anything here."

"Everything was perfect less than two hours ago. I don't understand."

"I know, man. I wish I could help you. Go on. Get out of here. Something tells me she's going to stay in there for a long time. Just go home. Something is bound to happen one way or the other."

I don't want to go home. I want to go into the building and demand answers. I want Jackson or Andy or someone to wheel my chair up I don't care how many flights of stairs so I can confront her.

That won't be the best thing for her and it definitely sure as hell won't be the best thing for me. It's bad enough that I'm this broken up over a woman who obviously doesn't want me.

I get Andy to drive me home. He goes straight to his apartment without a word. He doesn't try to reassure me or comfort me. He just evaporates which is exactly what I need right now.

I go to my apartment and do the hardest workout of my life. I want to forget everything, especially her and the last several weeks we've been together. I want to forget all of it, but everything reminds me of her now.

I won't even be able to walk into work without something reminding me of her. I'll have to deal with all the people who didn't want her around and who are thrilled that she's gone.

I won't be able to rely on her vision anymore. I'll have to come up with one of my own—which won't be anywhere near as good as hers.

I get out of the pool, put my clothes on, and go downstairs to make dinner. I can't even get excited about that. I want to be cooking for two to do something nice for her.

I can't even say I'm better off without her because I'm not. I am definitely better with her. My life is in the toilet without her. I don't even know where I would begin to find someone like her or anything even somewhat close to being as good as what I had with her.

I make dinner and eat it even though my heart isn't in it. I should just go to bed and be done with it, but I don't think I could even sleep. I'll just lie there dwelling on all of this.

She accepted me. She started a life with me even knowing everything that's wrong with me and everything I did wrong in the past. She showed me that I was attractive and appealing and even irresistible.

She showed me what love is—both to give it and to receive it. How am I ever supposed to replace that? I can't.

I clean up the kitchen. I'm just turning off the lights to go upstairs when the apartment door lock clicks. It opens from the outside even though it was locked a second ago.

Mila comes in still holding her electronic code card. She takes one look at me and looks away.

I sit in one place staring at her as she crosses the room and sits on the couch facing the windows and the terrace. She always loved that view, but she looks heartbroken now. I can't think of any other reason except that she must be coming back here to break up with me.

She doesn't say anything or even look at me. She sits there with her back to me. I can't stand the anticipation. I just want to get the break over with.

I roll over there and park my chair in front of her where she has no choice but to face me. "Is it over, baby?" My voice cracks. "Is that what's going on? Did you come back here to end it with me? Just tell me the truth. Don't play games with me."

She looks up at me and tears well up in her eyes. My stomach drops into my shoes and then, without warning, she buries her face in her hands and bursts into loud, wailing sobs.

I stare at her in stunned disbelief. Why would she dump me if she's this upset about it? Why would she dump me at all if she doesn't want to?

I swallow hard trying to come up with something to say, but she doesn't give me a chance. She turns aside, opens her purse, pulls out a folded piece of paper, and hands it to me.

The letterhead at the top says, *Seventh Avenue Optometrists, Inc.* That's the office she went to for her appointment.

I keep reading down the page and my world crumbles through my fingers.

Bietti's crystalline dystrophy (BCD) is a rare genetic condition that usually appears in the teen years and early twenties. BCD causes fatty acids crystals to develop and accumulate in the cornea and retina of the eye, which causes degradation of vision, beginning with difficulty seeing in low light conditions and in the peripheral vision. The condition eventually leads to impaired vision and eventual blindness. There is currently no known treatment for this condition.

I stare at the page reading it again and again trying to come to terms with what it's saying. She can't possibly have this....can she?

She got this paper at the optometrist's appointment. They wouldn't have given it to her if she didn't have the condition.

This is the only explanation for why she's so upset—and why she's been staying away from me all day. She's going blind. She will eventually go completely blind. This is the end of her photography career—the only career she ever wanted to do.

That word strikes a red-hot dagger into my heart. Blindness. She'll go blind. She won't be able to see anything. She won't be able to continue helping direct Mammoth Media's artistic vision. She won't be able to do anything she did before.

I look up. She sits there bowed, broken, and sobbing her eyes out in front of me. This is the worst disaster I can possibly imagine. It's catastrophic—and I can't do anything to stop it.

I pivot my chair over to the couch, hoist myself onto the cushion next to her, and pull her into my arms.

I can't even say anything to her. I can't tell her how much I love her. I can't tell her how special and precious and talented she is. I can't remind her of the thousands or maybe even millions of lives she's already touched and improved and saved.

None of that means anything right now because she's losing everything that ever meant anything to her. I don't know what's going to happen to her, but I just have to be here for her—as long as she'll let me.

She completely falls apart as soon as I put my arms around her. I don't even have to tell her that I read the paper and I understand what she's going through. This is so much worse than me getting hit by a car.

I didn't lose my company when I got hit by a car. I didn't lose my livelihood or my passion or my career. I didn't really lose anything except the ability to hit on girls I didn't even care about.

She collapses against me shaking with anguish. I let my lips sink onto her hair and tip back on the couch to pull her onto my chest.

I can't do anything except be this. I'm the chest she cries on. That's all I'm good for and that's enough. I don't need anything else as long as she's here.

Chapter 25: Mila

I wake up in the middle of the night and blink at the lights of New York shining through the window. It takes me a minute to realize where I am and why.

I'm in Giovanni's apartment, but I'm not in bed. We're lying on the couch. Then I remember and I can't stop the tears from welling up again. I'll lose my vision. I'm going to go blind. There is no cure.

Giovanni's arms close around me. His hand rubs up and down my back, massages my neck, and he runs his fingers through my hair endlessly, silently. He's always there and he never says a word to comfort me or make it okay.

It isn't okay. It will never be okay. I won't even be able to see my own photographs that I'm so proud of. I'll never be able to see the faces of the people I've helped.

I cry myself to sleep again. I'm already too exhausted to function. My exhaustion makes me more emotional than I already am.

I get woken up the next morning by a phone ringing. It's Giovanni's. He tries to sit up without disturbing me. I roll off him to the side so he can get it out of his pocket.

He takes the call still lying on his back. "Hello?" he mumbles. "Yeah. Yeah. Yeah, I know. I had a family emergency last night. I know. I'm on my way now. Just deal with it, okay, Cal? I said I'm on my way."

He hangs up and stares at the screen.

"You better go," I mumble.

He puts his phone down and turns to me. "I want you to come with me. We're having a meeting of the creative team for the Golden Road campaign and I think you should be there. You aren't blind yet. You can still make a difference for as long as your vision lasts. Maybe something will come up in the meantime and you'll see a new path for yourself."

I look away and grumble, "I don't want to deal with any of this."

"I know, sweetie. None of us does, but this is the situation in which we find ourselves. Come back to the office with me. Dante is off his nut over this campaign and you still have enough vision to see that through, at least. You don't have to do anything more than that, but I think it's important for you to stay on the horse and keep riding it as long as you can. Don't quit because of this."

I don't want to listen to him. He doesn't give me a chance. He sits up, pulls his wheelchair toward him, and pivots his body into it. He goes to the bathroom, brushes his teeth, straightens his hair, and calls Andy to drive him to the office.

Giovanni takes my hand at the door. "Come with me. You don't have to do anything. You can just sit there in silence if you want to. Just come with me. You shouldn't stay alone right now. Let me at least be there for you even if you don't do anything."

I can't deny him when he talks like that. He places my hand on his shoulder and we walk out of the apartment together. Andy doesn't say anything when we meet him at the elevator. He doesn't act at all surprised to see me.

We drive to the office and go upstairs to the fortieth floor. I sit at the table while the other department heads and directors gather to discuss the project.

They start out by complaining about it until Giovanni tells them that we aren't here to discuss if we will or won't go ahead with the new concept. He says the decision has already been made and their only task is to execute it to the highest standard.

All the complaining stops when Dante and some of his marketing people show up. He's more enthusiastic than ever and can't wait to roll out the campaign.

I find myself looking at the pictures I've come up with. I'm proud of them. I get a rush of gratitude that I can actually see these pictures. I don't know how much longer that will last.

Giovanni is right. I should keep doing this as much as I can. I might actually be able to do some good somewhere along the line.

Next we go to a different meeting with the fashion department. Sanders is there rolling out his latest ideas for all the new projects he has lined up.

He hooks up his laptop to the screen on the wall behind him. He runs a slideshow of some preliminary sketches, designs, and concept shots he's done to convey the idea behind his plans.

I find myself squinting at the screen. I can't make out some of the details no matter how hard I strain. I keep my mouth shut about his ideas. I can't even see them.

Giovanni takes me back to the lounge room afterward and pulls out a dozen folders of pictures, both hand-drawn and photographed.

"I want you to spend as much time as you can going over some of our upcoming projects," he tells me. "I don't want you to deal with the day-to-day, nuts-and-bolts operation of how this is all going to work out. I want you to focus on concept and artistic vision."

I shake my head and push the folders back at him. "I don't think this is a good idea. I couldn't even see Sanders' designs. My vision is deteriorating so much faster than I realized." I choke on the words. "I don't think I should be here at all."

"Of course you should. The vision in your head is the most important thing even if you're completely blind. Don't you get it? You have it all up there in your head. It's just a question of getting it out into the world. Come on. Don't give up."

He tries to take my hand, but I pull away. "I don't know how to do any of this. I don't even know if I can have a relationship with you anymore. I don't know who I am without this."

He slumps in his chair. "Do you want to have a relationship with me? Just tell me that much."

"Of course I do." I choke on tears. I can't hold them back. "I just don't know how to."

"Okay," he breathes. "Just do whatever you have to do. I'll handle this. You don't have to stay here if you don't want to. Just.....just know that I love you and I always will. I'll do anything I can to help you. I just want what's best for you and for you to be happy, even if that means we can't be together."

I can't stand to hear him talk like that. I want to be with him more than anything. It tears my heart out that I can't be—not like this.

I walk out of the office and immediately start crying again. I shouldn't be walking away from him. Walking away from him feels all wrong, but I don't know what else to do.

I don't want Andy to drive me anywhere in a big fancy limo. I don't want to do any of this. I just want my life to go back to the way it was before, but it won't. It will never go back to the way it was before—not ever.

I set off walking through town. I have nowhere to go, nowhere to be, no one waiting for me. I don't want to see anyone I know or talk to anyone. I want to disappear.

I wind up back at my old apartment building. At least I can be alone here, but I realize my mistake as soon as I get upstairs.

The door creaks open like I'm walking into a haunted mansion that no one has lived in for a hundred years. The place doesn't feel like I ever lived here—or like anyone has ever lived here.

My photography studio occupies most of the living room. I never use it as a living room. I wanted it to look professional when people came over for shoots. I didn't want them to realize that I actually lived here.

I converted the bedroom into my living space with the bed on one side and a couch and small coffee table on the other. That's where I actually lived when I wasn't using the kitchen and bathroom. I used the rest of the apartment for my business.

My photography equipment, books, and supplies crowd every shelf and surface. My photography surrounds me everywhere I look. What a vicious betrayal that turned out to be. Photography is the only job I ever loved enough to do and now I'm losing it.

I hate this place. I never want to see it again. I walk out of the apartment and wind up back on the sidewalk. Now where am I supposed to go? I have nowhere else.

I absolutely refuse to go to my parents' place in Jersey. Hell no. They would treat me like a sick child. My life would become an even more pathetic defeat there than it is here.

Whatever I do, I have to do it on my own. I have to figure this out one way or the other.

Giovanni kept going with his career when he lost the use of his legs. I can't do that, but maybe I should follow his example and just keep going with what I can do. I just don't know what that would be.

Chapter 26: Mila

I turn away from my old apartment building to go to Central Park. I don't plan to do anything other than walk around and appreciate the sights while I can still see them. That's the best I can do for now.

I turn a corner and come face to face with Connor walking the other way. He freezes at the same time and we stand facing off against each other.

Is this the time when he's finally going to attack me? He attacked a man in a wheelchair. Connor is capable of anything if he's capable of that.

He recovers first and sneers at me. "Where's your rich boyfriend? Did he dump you already?"

Something clicks in my mind. I still have Giovanni. I still want to be with him. I just don't know how to be with him.

"No, he didn't dump me and I didn't dump him," I tell him. "We're still together. He just has to work and so do I. Have a great day, Connor. Don't forget we still have a restraining order against you."

I walk off toward the park. Connor isn't worth my time. Giovanni is the one who has been there for me—and he still wants to be with me.

He would still want to be with me even if I was totally blind. He would accept that exactly the same way I accepted his disability. What the hell difference does it make when we know each other so well?

I walk around the park until the sun goes down. I would stay out a lot later. I want to spend every day here until I can't see anything at all anymore.

Maybe even then I'll want to come out here and just listen to all the noises. I suppose the world is still a beautiful place. Blind people do it all the time. I guess I have no reason not to do the same thing.

I'm still not ready to go back to Giovanni's apartment and face reality. Maybe this is just my deep funk over the disappointment of it all. Maybe I'm just wallowing in self-pity and I need to get over myself already.

I head to the Nova Gallery instead. I have nothing else to do.

The gallery is open tonight. Someone else is having an opening, but the gallery isn't as crowded. I walk in and wander from one display to another. I turn a corner near the Infection display and stop. Giovanni sits there in front of the pictures staring at one at his eye level.

Then he moves his wheelchair to another spot and stares at another picture for a long time. He works his way down the wall one picture at a time.

I could search for an eternity and never find a man who accepts me the way he does. I could search for an eternity and never find a man who cares for me as much as he does.

He just wants me. He doesn't care if I'm blind. I would never find that again—in anyone.

I walk over to him. He barely glances up at me before he goes back to looking at the pictures. "I didn't know you were going to be here," he murmurs. "I wouldn't have come if I had known. I know you want to be alone. I didn't come to intercept you."

"Why did you come?"

"These pictures......They make me feel close to you. I just wanted to be near you—and this was the closest I could get. I'll leave if you want me to. I don't want you to come to me if you don't want me."

"I do...I just......"

He turns around and looks up at me. It's the same old thing. I want him. I just don't know how to cross that bridge. He's always done that for me before. He always made it so much easier.

I glance around at all the pictures. "I don't even recognize these pictures. They don't seem to belong to me anymore. They look like they were taken by someone else." I sigh and face the wall in front of me. "I don't even know who I am."

He wheels closer, stops at my side, and slips his hand into mine. "I know who you are. Come home with me and I'll help you figure it out. You need me right now. You shouldn't go through this alone. There's no need for you to. You say you want to be with me but you don't know how. Then be with me not knowing how. We'll figure it out. We said we would face whatever came together. We'll face this, too. You're still the same person. You're still in there. The person who did all of this didn't suddenly disappear while you were at the optometrist's office. You don't know what the future holds and neither do I, but it will still be you—and me. That doesn't have to change. You say you don't want it to and it won't. It might even make us stronger." He squeezes my hand. "Come home with me. You don't have to be out here wandering alone. That's no way to deal with this."

I can't even look at him. I can't see anything through these tears.

He puts my hand on his shoulder. I'm already blind from these tears, but it's okay because he's here. I still have him—and that's a lot. It's much more than I could have asked for.

He wheels out of the gallery. I don't have to cope. I just have to go with him and let him guide me.

He doesn't call Andy to come and get us. We set walk all the way uptown back to his building. We walk the whole way in silence, take the elevator up to the penthouse, and he lets me in. I still have my key, but I still feel like a guest.

I sit down on the couch and he moves over to sit next to me. He doesn't put his arm around me. He doesn't try to kiss me. He doesn't even try to talk to me.

He just sits there. He doesn't have to do anything except be there. He's right. I can't stand going through this alone—and I don't have to. He'll always be there.

He does so much more than accept me. His scars—his legs—my scars—they're all superficial. I don't love him for his body. I love him for the person he is. So why can't he do the same thing?

I won't be able to see just like he can't walk. I'll have a disability and I'll have to do things differently from other people. So what? That will just be the way we do things.

I don't know how to have a relationship with him, but I do still feel like I belong with him. Maybe that's one of the things we'll have to do differently—kind of like the way he gets into a pool.

He gets on his phone, navigates around for a while, and asks, "Chinese or Italian for dinner tonight?"

I shrug. "Chinese, I guess."

He makes a call, places an order for both of us, and calls down to the doorman in the building lobby to tell him we're expecting a delivery. Then Giovanni goes back to sitting in silence.

I study him and find myself looking around at the apartment. Part of me feels like I've never been here before, either. I have to learn a whole new way of living here—and I'll have to learn a whole new way of living here when I lose my sight, too.

He gets another phone call from his doorman, switches back to his wheelchair, and goes down to the lobby to get the food. He comes back and lays everything out on the coffee table in front of me.

"Can I ask you a question?" I ask after we start eating.

"Sure. Fire away."

"How did you learn to do all of this? How long were you in the hospital before you started learning how to do all of this?"

"I recovered from the surgery in four months. The doctors pinned up all the broken bones. Then I went into rehab and it all started from there."

"So how long were in you rehab?"

He makes a face. "A year. I ran my business from my hospital bed and then I started with the wheelchair at about the six-month mark. It took a long time for me to build up my strength so I could move around. It took even longer before I could move around easily. That was the hardest part. I used to get so frustrated that I wasn't strong enough to move around as easily as I wanted to. That's what made me channel all my frustration into working out and getting stronger. It pissed me off so bad that I couldn't do what I wanted."

I look down at my food. "I guess that's what I'll have to do. I'll have to go to rehab."

"That's one way of looking at it. It's just bad luck that you have a career that absolutely requires that you be able to see—and not just see but see clearly. It isn't like that for me. I would still be able to use a computer and read spreadsheets and hold meetings and tell people what to do if I went blind. I didn't stop being able to do all those things just because I wound up in a wheelchair."

I can't look at him. "I just don't know what I'm going to do."

"You don't have to know. You'll figure it out and it's okay even if you don't. You've already made a massive contribution to society and won awards for it. You've changed countless lives. That's what you have to remember. Anything you do after this will just be dessert."

I laugh—or I try to. "Very funny."

He leans across the table and takes my hand. "I mean it, sweetheart. You're already a success by any measure. You couldn't become any more successful if you tried. Everyone admires and respects you. They admire and respect you a thousand times more than they respect me. I'm the luckiest guy in the world just to be sitting here eating Chinese food with you. You're going to be just fine. You have nothing to prove to me, the world, or yourself. You've already done a thousand times more than most people do in their lifetimes. Just remember that."

I don't want to listen to him even though I know he's right about that, too. I can be proud of my accomplishments. "I just need a direction to go in," I mumble. "I don't know where to go or what to do."

"Then come back to Mammoth until you figure it out. It isn't like you have to stay there forever. It's a direction to go in until you decide to change to something else. It's simple. You just go where your heart tells you to go—and if it isn't telling you where to go right now, then you have no reason *not* to go, do you?"

Chapter 27: Giovanni

I glance over at Mila sitting on the limo seat next to me, but she doesn't look at me. She stares through the window at the Mammoth Media building coming closer down the block.

She doesn't smile or get excited or even scared by the thought of going in there. I had to practically drag her out the door this morning.

She probably won't participate in any of our meetings or projects. Maybe I made a mistake by encouraging her to come back here.

I just don't want her sitting at home moping and waiting for her eyesight to fail completely. I wouldn't be doing her justice if I let her do that.

Andy drops us off. I get into my wheelchair and Mila and I go upstairs to the office. She sits to one side staring out the window at the skyline.

"Come over here and take a look at these projects for me," I tell her. "You aren't blind yet. You can give me your opinion on them."

She drags her chair over and rolls her eyes at me, but she fights back a smirk while she does it. She knows she's moping. At least she can make fun of herself for doing it.

I lay out the projects in front of her and she flips through them. Then she asks me for a pen and a piece of paper. I don't have one, so I give her my tablet with an open notetaking app on it.

She does a few sketches. "I think this would be better....and I think you should change this to a winter scene—not a summer one."

I nod and take notes on what she's telling me.

She flips a few more pages. "I don't think you should go for this industrial, car-enthusiast vibe on this one. I think you should go for a soft, wholesome, family vibe."

I shrug. "Okay. Good idea."

She turns to the next one, and right then, one of the designers walks in with a different folio of pictures.

The designer puts it down in front of me and starts telling me about how they're inking the machines to start printing the marketing material for a different campaign later this afternoon.

I nod and open the folder. The pictures look great. Mila bends over and points to one of them. "Don't you think it would look better if you increased the saturation on that one?"

"It's already as saturated as it can get," the designer tells her.

Mila doesn't look up or respond. She stares down at the picture for a minute and then rushes out of the room.

I let her go. It's going to be like this for a long time. She might even quit again. She might even quit dozens of times. I'll just have to live with that and so will she.

I continue with the rest of my appointments for the morning. She'll probably just go straight back home after this latest defeat. She didn't want to come in anyway.

I wait until lunchtime before I call her. I plan to ask her to meet me for lunch somewhere outside the building. She doesn't answer her phone. Not this again.

I consider calling Andy next to go to my apartment and tell her to answer her goddamn phone for Christ's sake, but at the last second, I decide to check my GPS to see if she even did go home. I frown at the screen when I see that she's still in the building.

I expand the image and motor through the building until I track down the signal. It's coming from the music department. I don't know what I'll find over here or what in the world could have brought her here.

I stop outside one of the recording studios and stare at my phone for a minute. Her signal is coming from inside. She still has her phone with her and it's still turned on. So why doesn't she answer?

I go into the sound booth half-expecting her to be sitting in on one side listening to the recording session.

The engineers look up when I roll into the room. One of them even shoots out of his chair to get to his feet. "Oh, sorry, Mr. Nowaczyk! We weren't expecting you!" the guy blurts out.

"Take it easy, fellas," I tell them. "I'm just...."

I freeze when I hear the voice coming through the mixing board and speakers in the room. The voice is coming from the studio behind the glass.

I turn around and see Mila sitting at a piano on the other side of the glass. She's playing the piano and singing into the microphone in front of her. She wears a pair of thick headphones over her ears and she has her eyes closed.

"Can we help you with something, Mr. Nowaczyk?" one of the other engineers asks.

"Are you guys recording this?"

"Sure," the first guy replies. "We were just finishing recording Sheila Templeton for the day. She left and this girl came in and asked us if we minded if she used the piano. We said we didn't mind because we still had work to do. She started singing and playing and we told her to hold up so we could record it. Can you believe it? She's never done anything professionally before—and she sounds a hell of a lot better than Sheila." The guy glances at me. "Don't tell anyone I said that."

I can't even respond. Mila sings her heart out into the microphone—and she does sound better than Sheila Templeton.

Mila sings a song of heartbreak, loss, and pure, agonized longing for the love she once knew. She sings in a deep, soulful tone cracking with buried emotion and genuine feeling. The sound and the words send goosebumps down my arms.

She keeps pouring her heart out until she comes to the end of the refrain. She opens her eyes to play the last chords on the piano. I never even knew she played the piano. She never mentioned it as part of her life.

One of the engineers presses the monitor button on the soundboard. "That was awesome, Mila," he tells her. "Why don't you come in and lay down a few more tracks tomorrow and we can talk about doing your next number?"

She smiles at him through the glass—and then she sees me sitting there. I can't read her eyes. Is she angry that I burst in here and found her doing this?

She pulls off her headphones, pushes back the piano stool, and leaves the studio through a side door. I turn my wheelchair around to go meet up with her.

"Mr. Nowaczyk?" the engineer asks. "Should we....should we keep recording her?"

"Yes, absolutely. Keep doing it as long as she wants. We should cultivate her and maybe produce her. Get her to lay down as much material as she wants—as much as she feels comfortable with. Let me know if you need anything else—and let me know once you get enough material to actually produce. We could even release that one as a single. I'll send you down the details tomorrow."

I leave the sound booth just as Mila comes out of the studio. "What the hell is going on?" I ask. "I was looking for you all over the building."

"You won't believe it, Giovanni!" she blurts out, and before I can even move, she jumps onto my lap, sits on me sideways, and throws her arms around my neck to kiss me.

"Hey!" I push her back. "What's going on here?! You never said you were into music!"

"I'm not! I mean…I wasn't…..but I am! Don't you see?"

"No, I don't see because you haven't explained anything to me. You ran off and I thought you went home."

"I was going to! I ran off and I broke down crying in the hallway. I really was going to quit for real, but I took a walk around the building just to calm down before I went back to tell you that it really was over this time. I was walking past that studio and I heard a woman singing in there…."

"Her name is Sheila Templeton. She's a Grammy-winning singer."

She waves that away. "That doesn't matter because the song just…. well, I don't know what happened. I only heard it for a split second and this other song just popped into my head out of nowhere. I mean—all the lyrics and everything just….happened. I don't understand it. It just happened. I went into the booth over there and she was just leaving. I asked those guys if I could use the piano and I sat down and started playing and singing the song in my head…."

"You never told me you play the piano! Why didn't you tell me?"

"I don't play the piano—I mean not anymore. My parents made me take lessons when I was younger, but that's all. I gave it up when I discovered photography. I haven't played in years, but it all came back like it was meant to be. I didn't understand it—and then those guys asked if they could record the song." She blinks at me. "Don't be mad at them. They were really nice about it."

"I'm not mad. I'm just...surprised."

"It's like you said. I have this.....this thing in my head.....and it doesn't matter if I can see or not. I guess you could say that whatever it was that I did with the Infection Project is still in there and needed another way to come out. It was perfect....at least....I think it went w ell."

"It did. It sounded great—and the guys loved it."

She leans all the way against me, runs her fingers through my hair, and kisses me with all the slow, sultry passion I used to know before all this whole nightmare happened.

"I can't wait to start learning more instruments and writing more songs," she murmurs. "This is going to be perfect. Remember when you said I should just keep going in one direction until I found out what other direction I wanted to take? This is it. I'm certain of it. I can't wait to do this. It's exactly what I need."

I want to question her more about this, but the energy buzzing through her is like nothing I've ever felt. She throws herself at me and barely stops herself from squirming against my body.

She rubs her breasts on my chest and screws her hips down onto my lap. She does it until she makes me start to get hard.

I have to tear my lips away from her so I can see where I'm going. "Hold on," I tell her. "We aren't doing this in the middle of the hallway."

She squeals in excited glee when I drive away in the other direction and push open the door to another studio. No one is using this one.

I drive her into the sound booth and lock the door. She bursts out in thrilling giggles when I turn around and grab her.

She comes at me even harder and attacks me kissing me like never before. She's on fire. I paw her all over. Every touch excites her more. I slip my hand between her legs and she shivers with explosive tension.

She moans and I pull her back and forth on my knob. I want her right now—right this minute.

She arches her back into me. I grab her shirt, tear it down, and snatch her breast in my mouth. She yelps and then screams while I rub her between her legs. She's making me so hard I can't stand it.

I grab her pants and tear her fly open so I can plunge my hand down inside her panties. Her wetness swallows my hand up to my knuckles. I have to have her. I can't let this moment pass us by.

She grabs my belt and starts yanking it loose while I scoot her panties down her hips. I only get them as far as her thighs before I scoop her up. I can't wait a second longer.

I barely rip my fly open in time to lower her onto my rigid shaft. She screams into my mouth and convulses in my arms, but I won't let her go. I raise and lower her to my own rhythm.

She spasms again and again and then falls whimpering, sobbing, and gasping on my shoulder. I'm nowhere near done with her. I sit her up, turn her backward, and push her legs to straddle me facing the other way.

She flops and barely holds herself upright. I take hold of her arms and pull her back into my thrusts. She responds perfectly, bursts into a frenzy of bucking and moaning, and rides me to another blistering climax before I unload inside her.

I pull her back into my arms as soon as it's over, turn her sideways, and cradle her while she rests on my shoulder. I needed that so badly—and so did she.

We still got it. She's still mine—and now she's on the other side of that dark place where she doesn't know what she's living for.

Chapter 28: Giovanni

I stroke Mila's delicious body until she calms down. I'm in no hurry to leave and go back to work. She's more important.

She finally sits up on my lap, sniffs, and rubs her eyes. "Are you okay, baby?" I ask.

She nods. "I....I think I better go home. I can still be involved in the company as long as it's in a capacity that doesn't require me to see anything."

"I would still like to get your input on things for as long as your vision lasts...but maybe we could do that at home so you don't have to do it in front of other people."

"Okay," she mumbles. "I could do that."

"Would you like to get involved in the music department?" I ask. "Apart from recording your own stuff?"

"I guess I could. I don't have any reason not to."

"Let's see how it goes. Do you want me to call Andy to come and get you?"

"I think I need to walk. I want to think about a few things on the way." She drags her bleary eyes open and smiles at me for the first time. "Thank you for that. I really needed that."

"Anytime you say, you just let me know. I'll find a way to service you."

She laughs, climbs off me, and pulls up her pants. "I'll remember that."

I walk her out to the lobby and take her hand. "Did you turn your phone to *Do Not Disturb* when you went into the studio?"

"Oh! I completely forgot!" She takes out her phone, turns it back on, and stares at the screen. "I missed a few calls from you."

"Just stay in touch with me, okay? I don't want to start worrying about you again."

She kisses me. "I'm sorry. I won't do it again. I'm going to walk straight home from here. I'll see you when you get there."

"Okay, sweetie. I'm really glad you found this. It's gonna be so good for you."

She bursts into a grin. "I can't wait."

I somehow get through the rest of the workday and pry myself out of the building so I can go home. God only knows what will be waiting for me when I get there.

I get another prickle up my scalp when I get out of the elevator and hear Mila's voice coming through the open penthouse door. She's playing the guitar this time and singing a completely different song.

I halt in my tracks to listen. She sings with the same haunted, cracked quality of broken emotion that I heard in the studio.

She stops midsentence, mutters something under her breath, and then starts over from the beginning only to stop at the same spot.

Andy and I exchange glances. He raises his eyebrows at me before he splits off to his own apartment. This one is all mine to deal with.

I hesitate to go into the penthouse. I know I have to, but I don't want to interrupt her. I want her to keep going. She must be waiting for me if she left the door open for me.

Right then, she walks into view and does something in the kitchen. She's making something in the oven and she pulls open the door to check it.

She's carrying a guitar in her left hand. It looks new.

I roll into the room and shut the penthouse door behind me. She brightens up right away. "Hey, sweetie!" she greets me.

"Hey, baby," I remark. "Did you buy that guitar on the way home?"

"Yeah!" She bursts out in excited laughter. "I only learned a few chords in high school—so I have some catching up to do—and I got an electric piano to practice with. I hope you don't mind."

"I don't mind at all. I want you to explore this as much as possible."

She comes over to hug and kiss me. "How was your day?"

"It was great. I banged this really hot photographer in the back room. She was really juicy and responsive and her tits were outstanding...."

She bursts out laughing and walks away from me blushing. "I'm sure you made her scream with delight."

"Oh, I did—twice."

She sits down on the couch, puts the guitar across her knee, and strums a few chords, but she stops and laughs again. "Now I can't concentrate. Thanks a lot."

I can't help but grin at her. "You aren't going to be able to use our sex life as an excuse to get distracted. Pay attention to what's important."

"Which one are you referring to—music or our sex life?"

"Both. Pay attention to whichever one you're doing at the time."

"Well, now I'm trying to work out this song and you're distracting me with our sex life."

"I'm not distracting you with anything of the kind. I'm on the opposite side of the room. You asked me how my day went and I told you the truth—but I could distract you with our sex life if you really want me to."

She blushes again and puts the guitar down. Now I see the electric piano on the dining room table. She picks it up and tilts it against the wall so she can start setting our places for dinner.

I go into the living room. She's scribbled miles and miles of chicken scratch on a notepad, torn the pages off, and laid them out in a messy grid pattern on the coffee table.

She's blacked out different sections, drawn arrows between certain blocks of text and others, and rewritten notes into the margins.

"No peeking," she calls from the kitchen. "It's still in the rough, embarrassing stages."

"I can't read your handwriting. You don't have to worry about me seeing anything."

She laughs again. "Good. That will be my unbreakable code."

"I'm gonna hear the song anyway because you'll be singing it in front of me. In fact, I already did hear you."

She turns bright red. "I'll improve it. I swear."

"It already sounds amazing—and that song you did in the studio was amazing, too. You're a natural at this."

"You're sweet to say so."

I roll over to her and interrupt her work by taking her hand. "Listen to me, sweetheart. I'm your biggest fan. I'm not saying that because I'm trying to flatter you. I really mean it. The company could produce you. You could have a career—a real career that wouldn't require you to see anything. You're good enough. Why do you think the engineers asked to record you? You're better than Sheila Templeton. Even the engineers said so."

She starts to say, "Naw...." and pull her hand out of mine.

I tighten my grip on it. "Marry me, Mila. I love you and I want you to be mine forever. Marry me and live happily ever after with me. Don't ever leave. Depend on me and let me depend on you. We can build a future together. We have all the essential ingredients. All you have to do is say yes."

She blinks at me. "You're serious."

I pull the ring box out of my pocket. "I was going to propose to you before you found out about your vision loss. I held off because you got so upset and confused about it. I wanted to give you some time to come out of it."

I crack the box open, pull the ring out of its nest, and hold it close to her hand. "Will you marry me?"

Her eyes flood with tears and she turns away with a pained grimace. "I don't deserve you, Giovanni!" she chokes. "I let you down so many times."

I slip the ring onto her finger and pull her down on my lap. "You never let me down. You had a right to go a little off the rails when you found out about your eyes. Everything is going to be okay. I swear it."

She wraps her arms around me and nestles into my shoulder. She doesn't tell me to take the ring off and she doesn't say she won't marry me.

She sniffles on my shoulder for a second and then stands up way too fast. "Well! Someone has to make dinner around here if you're going to be out there banging photographers all the time."

Now it's my turn to laugh. "I might find a musician who looks good, too."

She laughs and wipes her hand across her cheeks while she checks whatever is in the oven. She's walking around with my ring on her finger and she's still over there making dinner. It looks like we're engaged.

Chapter 29: Mila

I pick up my cane as the limo door opens. I hear the familiar clink of Giovanni's wheelchair when Andy unfolds it on the sidewalk outside.

I listen to the sounds of Giovanni's movements as he sets his board across the two seats, slides himself across, and the wheelchair creaks when his weight sinks into it.

"Lift your feet, Ma'am," Andy tells me and he puts the board back into its place against the lower seat in front of me.

"Thank you, Andy," I tell him.

He takes my hand, helps me climb out of the car, and steers me over to Giovanni so I can find his shoulder to rest my hand on him.

Giovanni thanks Andy, too. "Do you want me to go home?" Andy asks. "I can find a place to wait for you."

"You don't have to," Giovanni tells him. "Go on home. I'll call you when we're ready to leave."

"Yes, Sir," Andy replies. "You two have a nice evening."

"Good night, Andy," I call after him.

"Good night, Ma'am. I'll see you in a few hours."

"Are you ready?" Giovanni asks me while I unfold my cane.

"I'm ready." I rest my hand on Giovanni's shoulder and he heads into the hotel lobby on his way to the ballroom for another Billionaires' Club gala.

I hear the noise long before we get there. I can see flashes of light in different places, but I can't make out anything distinct.

A sea of noise pulses out of the ballroom as we approach the entrance. "Wow," Giovanni breathes. "You should see this place, baby. It's like a Christmas tree come to life and all the sparkly people are the ornaments."

I laugh. "I bet they are. Who's here?"

"Everyone is here. Oh, there's Diego Rivera. I want to talk to him about that new company he just acquired."

"Don't go leading me into all your business conferences," I tell him. "Where are the women?"

"Women! Who said anything about women? I'm here to talk to my friends—and don't go telling me where to lead you. For a second I thought you were going to tell me not to lead you not into temptation—and we all know what I think of that."

I laugh again and squeeze his shoulder. "Stop it. We're in public here."

"When did that ever stop me?"

He stops his wheelchair just then and I hear Kevin Drake talking to Giovanni and then to me. "Hey, good-looking!" I can't tell if Kevin means me or Giovanni. "You two look outstanding together. Look at you, Mila! You look better than ever. Married life certainly agrees with you." He kisses me on the cheek. "I'm so glad you two made it."

Jackson Metcalf comes up to us just then, too, and then a bunch of women surround me. I recognize all their voices. I'm one of these women now. "Your new single was electric, Mila," Samantha tells me.

"What do you say to booking MegaDome for year after next?" Emberlynn asks me. "We need someone like you to balance out all the grunge metal."

"You'll have to consult my manager to make sure my other concert dates don't conflict—but other than that, yeah, I would love to play MegaDome."

"Is it true that Dante had another grandchild?" Vivian Salazar asks.

"That's ancient history, Vivian," Piper tells her. "What rock have you been living under?"

"She has kids," Emberlynn explains.

"You have kids," Piper points out.

"But I'm the step-grandmother. Of course I had to find out."

The others laugh. "Somehow you and the word, 'grandmother' don't belong in the same sentence," Samantha teases. "You're way too young."

Emberlynn joins in the joke. "I'm practicing for when my boys grow up and have kids. Don't ask me how I'm going to handle that."

"I'm sure you make a wonderful grandmother," Vivian remarks. "You're a natural with kids."

"When are you and Giovanni going to start, Mila?" Piper asks.

I turn bright red and pretend to glance around. "Is Giovanni anywhere within earshot?"

"I'm right here listening to your every word," his voice replies. "So when are we going to start, Mila?"

I wave that away. "Can we have that conversation in private?"

"No!" Piper counters. "Come on! We're all checking our watches and counting down the seconds."

I get flustered, but Niko Holloway's voice interrupts just then. "I'm going to steal your husband for a minute, Mila."

"He likes it gently, Niko—no rough stuff."

All the women burst out laughing and so do the men. Giovanni's voice fades into the crowd. I would feel more worried if I didn't have all these women around me, but they start to disperse pretty soon, too.

Some get called away to deal with their husbands. Others want to get food or drink.

Jackson materializes at my side, takes my hand, and slips it into my arm. "Can I escort you, Mrs. Nowaczyk?"

I blush and wind up giggling. "You're the first and only person who has ever called me that."

"Well, I'm honored to be the first, then." He sets off walking through the gala. "Are you hungry or thirsty? Where do you want to go?"

"I'm not hungry or thirsty. I just need to stay oriented until Giovanni comes back."

"We can just take a walk through the park. How does that sound?"

"Thank you. I really appreciate it."

"You and Giovanni are doing so well. We're all so proud of you both."

I beam at him. "Thank you. We couldn't have done it without all of you. I really appreciate your help in getting through our rough patches."

"Anything you need, you only have to call on us—or me—or whoever you feel like."

"I'm really grateful to you for being there for Giovanni when he needed you. I'm ashamed to think how badly I handled it."

"You didn't handle it badly at all. You handled it perfectly. Everything you did was perfectly appropriate. I'm sure any of us would have done the same thing."

I try to look away except that I can't see him. "I'm still grateful—and I'm grateful to you for taking care of me now. You've all been so kind and warm to us. We wouldn't want to do any of this without you."

"It's inspiring to see the way both of you have risen to the occasion. We're all honored and grateful to know you. It's nice to know we could get through it and thrive on the other end if something like that happened to one of us."

I squeeze his arm. "When are you going to settle down with someone?"

He chuckles. "Probably never. I'm married to my business."

"I don't believe you. A man as big-hearted as you has to find a woman to love eventually."

He pats my hand on his arm. "You're very sweet to say so. I'll let you know as soon as I find someone."

"You don't have to let me know. I just want you to be happy."

"I'll be lucky if I find someone who makes me as happy as you obviously make Giovanni. You two are a wonderful example to follow—especially considering what he was like before he met you."

I look away. "Everyone says that, but the truth is that he changed before he met me. I wouldn't have gotten together with him if he was like that."

"I know you're right. The accident woke him up and matured him. He never took anything seriously before—and now look at you two."

I smile and blush at him again, but Giovanni comes back before we can say anything else. "Do you mind if I cut in on your charming date, Jackson?"

"She's all yours, pal." Jackson pats my hand. "I'll see you around, Mila. Have a good evening."

"Thank you, Jackson." He walks away into the crowd and I rest my hand on Giovanni's shoulder. We make the rounds talking to all our friends.

It's hard to tear ourselves away at the end of the night, but we both eventually get too tired to stay. It takes a long time to say goodbye to everyone. Giovanni calls Andy to come and get us.

We wait in the hotel lobby until Andy calls back to tell us he's outside. Giovanni leads me out into the chilly night air. I hear traffic buzzing all around us and horns honking out of sight.

Giovanni stops me in the middle of the sidewalk. "Wait here, baby," he tells me. "Andy is trying to find a space to pull up to the curb. There's too much traffic....."

At that moment, a screech of tires rushes us from the right. I can't see anything in the dim light before the noise comes straight toward us.

A thump resounds through the pavement under my feet and an unstoppable force tears Giovanni away from me. A car skids on the pavement in front of me and a car screeches to a halt right where Giovanni should be.

I panic and try to reach around everywhere to find him. "Giovanni!!" I scream. "Giovanni—where are you!" I take a step forward and bump into the car.

A bunch of people start yelling and I hear sirens coming closer in the distance. I turn this way and that calling out for Giovanni, but I don't find him.

"Mila!!" His voice rasps somewhere on my left. He sounds like he's near the ground. "Mila....."

I stumble over there and my foot hits a body on the ground. I drop on my knees patting him down. His suit is soaking wet with something warm and sticky. "No!!" I moan. "No! Not again!"

"Mila......" he chokes. "Call....911....."

"I....I...." I pat down his jacket trying to find my phone. I put it in his inner jacket pocket to keep it safe. Now I can't find it. He can't have gotten hit by a car—not again.

Out of nowhere, Andy grabs me and pulls me away. "NO!!" I scream. "GIOVANNI!!"

"The ambulance is here!" Andy yells at me. "The medics are moving in to work on him! Come on! Get in the car, Mila! I'll drive you to the hospital."

That's the first time Andy has ever called me by my first name. He's always there. He always helps me and Giovanni with everything. We couldn't do any of this without him.

He wrestles me away. "The medics are with him," he tells me again. "We can't help him. Come on. We can't stay here."

He marches me through the crowd, opens a car door, and steers me into the seat of our own limo. He shuts the door with me inside.

Sitting here alone without Giovanni feels all wrong. He can't be hurt—not again—not after spending two years recovering and getting his life back.

He's been happier since we got together than he's ever been in his life. All his friends from the club say so. He's more energetic, more driven, more caring—more everything. I can't lose him. I need him more than anything.

I want to cry on the long trip to the hospital. That trip feels like it will last an eternity.

Andy finally pulls into a parking garage, takes me out of the seat, and leads me inside to the reception desk. He finds out where Giovanni is and Andy takes me upstairs to Giovanni's room. At least he isn't in surgery again.

A male doctor meets us there. "He has three cracked ribs. He's gonna be just fine. It could have been a whole lot worse."

"Is he....is he conscious?" I can barely say the words.

"He's awake and he's been asking for you. You can go in and see him now."

Andy leads me into the room and I pat down the bed until I feel Giovanni's bony legs under the blanket.

"Oh, thank God you're all right!" he husks from right in front of me. "I thought you might have gotten hurt, too."

"Are you.....?" I work my hands up the bed and accidentally touch his chest. He roars out in pain and convulses under my hand. "I'm so sorry! I was so worried!" I touch his face. "The doctors say you're going to be all right. You just have broken ribs."

"I'm all right, darling." He takes my hand, compresses it a few times, and guides it to his face.

I sit down on the edge of the bed and stroke his cheeks. His features feel so familiar. I can't stop touching him.

"I'm just so glad you're here," he breathes. "I'm glad I'm the one who got hit instead of you."

"Don't say that," I exclaim. "It shouldn't have happened to either of us."

He chuckles and ends by wincing again. "It just means you're going to have to wait on me hand and foot for the next few weeks while I heal up."

I can't help but smile at him. "I can definitely do that. Someone has to keep you serviced and your oil changed."

He starts to laugh and groans. "You can keep me serviced as long as you don't make me laugh."

I lean down and kiss him. I love him so much. "I'm going to tell Andy to go home. We're probably going to be here for a while."

"Okay, sweetheart. Just come back. I need you here."

"I need you, too. I wouldn't be anywhere else."

I touch his face just to reassure myself one last time before I stand up. I extend my cane in front of me to make sure I don't bump into anything on my way out of the room. At least I won't have to go too far. Andy will be waiting for me right out there in the hall.

I start to stand up when a rush of vertigo shoots to my head. I reel and almost fall over. Giovanni grabs my arm just in time to steady me. He pulls me back to sit down on the bed where I was before.

"Are you sure you're okay?" He rubs my back. "You said you didn't get hurt."

"I didn't. I just got really light-headed for a second. I don't know what happened." I cradle my head in my hand until the wave passes. "Maybe I'm just tired because it's late at night."

I hear a buzzing sound near the head of his bed. "Stay where you are," he tells me. "I'm going to call one of the nurses to take a look at you. I don't like where this is going."

I don't trust myself to stand up. Three different people come into the room and walk over to me. "What's going on?" a woman's voice asks.

"My wife just got really light-headed," Giovanni tells her. "She tried to stand up and almost fell over. I'm worried she either got hurt in the accident or there's something else wrong with her."

"Let's take a look." Someone tears some Velcro near my head. "I'm going to take your blood pressure, Ma'am. This will only take a minute."

The nurse starts strapping the blood pressure cuff around my arm. Another takes my pulse and sticks a clamp around my finger.

I groan and grab my head. "Aargh! It's coming back. I feel like I'm going to faint...."

Giovanni takes hold of my arm and pulls. "Lie down here, darling. Don't risk it."

He draws me down on the bed next to him. I wind up facing away from him into the room. He keeps rubbing my arms and stroking my hair.

"Her vitals all look good," one of the nurses remarks. "I'll inform the doctor and see about doing a blood draw."

The nurses leave me lying there with my head spinning. Giovanni never stops touching me. "Just don't expect me to wait on *you* hand and foot," he murmurs.

I want to laugh, but I'm feeling too out of it. I just lie there trying not to pass out while someone comes and takes a blood sample from me.

Andy's voice floats into my brain. "Is anything wrong, Mr. Nowaczyk?" he asks.

"That's what we're about to find out," Giovanni replies. "Do you need to go home or can you stick around for a minute?"

"I can stick around—at least long enough to find out if it's anything to worry about."

I don't hear anything else. It better not be anything to worry about. Giovanni and I have had enough bad news to last us the rest of our lives.

I must be slipping in and out of consciousness because I come back to my senses when I hear Giovanni talking to another woman. "It's nothing to worry about, Mr. Nowaczyk. Your wife is pregnant. She's about four weeks along—so this kind of dizziness isn't unusual. We usually see it around the time when the embryo implants in the uterine wall. The dizziness will pass pretty soon. We're releasing you, so you can...well, normally I would say she could take you home, but it looks more like you'll be taking her home. Congratulations. I'll send your release paperwork over for you to sign."

Giovanni says, "Thank you, Doctor," in a soft undertone. His voice trembles and then I hear Andy congratulating Giovanni, too.

"Do you hear that, darling?" Giovanni murmurs in my ear. "You're pregnant. We're going to have a baby. I love you so much. I hate to tell you this, but you're going to have to stand up and go out to the car. Can you do that?"

I drag myself into a sitting position. I still feel a little dizzy, but at least I can think straight now. I'm pregnant. I'm going to be a mother and Giovanni is going to be a father.

This is going to be a whole new adjustment to a new kind of life, but it's going to be wonderful. I can't wait.

I stay where I am and wait for my head to clear while the doctors and nurses release Giovanni from the hospital. He presses my hand. "Are you going to be okay?" he murmurs.

I turn to face him. "I'm going to be fine. I'll feel better after I get home and lie down for a while." I touch his cheeks. "I love you so much. I wouldn't want to do this with anyone else."

"Me, neither. You're going to be the best mother in history." He cups my cheeks and pulls my lips to his. I have to be careful not to touch him in certain places. I'm not used to that.

The nurses come back and Giovanni signs himself out. Then they put him in a hospital wheelchair to take him out of the hospital. He won't be pushing himself around for a while.

Andy comes over to me and takes my hand. "You better come with me, Ma'am," he tells me. "I'll walk you out to the car."

I take his arm with one hand and rest my other hand on Giovanni's shoulder. I don't want to get separated from him—not ever. All our dreams are coming true and we'll face them together, no matter what.

End of Book 6.

Keep Reading

The Billionaires' Club Series: Book 7: Last Hope

Billionaire industrial tycoon Jackson Metcalfe has always adored his long-time assistant McKenna Pearson. Both of their lives get thrown into chaos when she suddenly gets diagnosed with terminal leukemia and no way to know how much longer she has left to live. She quits her job to spend her last remaining days with her children. She's a single mother with no living relatives. Her children will have to go into foster care once she's gone.

Jackson can't stand to see the children's lives ruined any more than they already are. He steps in to help, which will lead all four of them down a harrowing path that can only end in McKenna's death. Neither Jackson nor McKenna knows how to handle it when their relationship starts to change with catastrophe hanging over their heads and time running out.

Nothing will prepare them for the inevitable outcome that will change the course of all their lives. Could this be the end of all their hopes and dreams or the start of something even better?

You can find it at your favorite book retailer.

Get All of
AE Moran's Free
Books

S ign Up Once—Get all A.E. Moran's free books including brand
  new releases

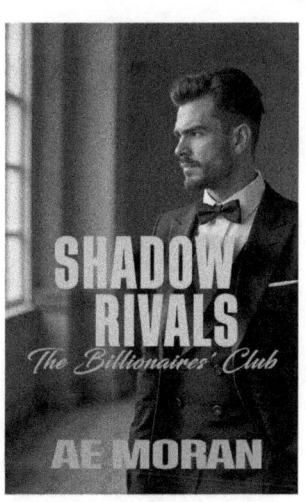

Holden Seager is hot, magnetic, and filthy, stinking, obscenely rich. He commands a room the minute he walks in the door. So what happens when meets another shark as powerful, as charismatic, and as successful as he is—not to mention ten years younger? When these two meet across the negotiating table, one of them will walk away the undisputed winner. The other will walk away with nothing.

Or so it seems.

Unless they're best friends.

When the business deal of a lifetime falls flat on its face and neither of these titans knows how to bring it back to life, this might be the opportunity Dayna Turner has been waiting for.

There's just one problem. She works as an assistant to one of these powerful men....and she's in love with the other. It's a recipe for disaster and heartbreak—unless Dayna can pull off an even bigger coup that will leave them all richer, happier, and more closely connected than ever. The alternative is the destruction of everything all three of them have worked so hard to build.

Sign up at www.authoraemoran.com to read it for free.

About AE Moran

A .E Moran is the contemporary romance pen name for Theo Mann.

I write 70 books per year—and yes, before you ask, all these books are my original creative work. Nothing written under my name is AI-generated or ghostwritten because I write better than AI and any ghostwriter out there.

People don't read fiction for entertainment or to escape from reality. People read fiction to see their humanity reflected in another person's character and story.

This is my promise to you. When you read my books, you'll see your own humanity reflected in the characters and stories. I take this commitment to my readers very seriously. My books are an intimate form of communication between us. I would never disrespect my readers by turning that over to a machine or another writer. This is my bond between me and you as my reader.

I write 20,000 words per day as my daily work output. If anyone with a public platform would like to challenge me to prove this in a controlled environment, feel free to contact me on this website's contact page.

I worked as a professional ghostwriter for fifteen years. Now I'm going for the Guinness World Record by writing 700 books over the next ten years and 1400 books over the next twenty years, all originally written by me. See my website for the full book list.

I'm also the author of *Proof for the Existence of God* and the *Crimes Against Fiction* blog. You can find all my nonfiction work at www.cr imes-against-fiction.com.

If you have a story idea, or if you would like me to explore a series in more depth, or if you'd like me to explore a character by writing a spinoff series about that character or world, leave me a message on my website's contact page. I answer all reader emails, so ask me anything, tell me what you liked and didn't like, and let me know where you'd like your favorite series to go. I would love to hear your ideas and find out what you'd like to read next.

You can find out more at www.theomann.com or at www.author aemoran.com.

Also by AE Moran (so far)

Standalone Novels

Heart on a Knife Edge

Dream Dimension

Just Friends

Back From the Dead

Damaged

Small Town Reunion

Series

Firehouse Blues (Books 1-10)

Turning Point Ranch (Books 1-10)

The Billionaires' Club (Books 1-10)

Paradise Cruises (Book 1-8)

Royal House (1-10)

Summerton Estates (1-10)